"Don't Misur I'm Going To *Baby. Not You.*

One light brown eyebrow lifted and Kathy's toes curled. Oh, brother, what was she letting herself in for?

"Strictly business?" he asked.

She cleared her throat noisily. "Business."

"Good. It's a deal, then," Brian said, and held out one hand.

She looked at it as if it were a snake and had to work up her nerve before she slid her hand into his. But even braced for the contact with his skin, as his fingers were curled around hers, she felt a white-hot burst of light shoot straight from her fingertips, along her arm to dazzle her heart.

She was in deep trouble. She could feel it in her bones.

Dear Reader,

In keeping with the celebration of Silhouette's 20th anniversary in 2000, what better way to enjoy the new century's first Valentine's Day than to read six passionate, powerful, provocative love stories from Silhouette Desire!

Beloved author Dixie Browning returns to Desire's MAN OF THE MONTH promotion with *A Bride for Jackson Powers,* also the launch title for the series THE PASSIONATE POWERS. Enjoy this gem about a single dad who becomes stranded with a beautiful widow who's his exact opposite.

Get ready to be seduced when Alexandra Sellers offers you another sheikh hero from her SONS OF THE DESERT miniseries with *Sheikh's Temptation.* Maureen Child's popular series BACHELOR BATTALION continues with *The Daddy Salute*—a marine turns helpless when he must take care of his baby, and he asks the heroine for help.

Kate Little brings you a keeper with *Husband for Keeps,* in which the heroine needs an in-name-only husband in order to hold on to her ranch. A fabulously sexy doctor returns to the woman he could never forget in *The Magnificent M.D.* by Carol Grace. And exciting newcomer Sheri WhiteFeather offers another irresistible Native American hero in *Jesse Hawk: Brave Father.*

We hope you will indulge yourself this Valentine's Day with all six of these passionate romances, only from Silhouette Desire!

Enjoy!

Joan Marlow Golan

Joan Marlow Golan
Senior Editor, Silhouette Desire

Please address questions and book requests to:
Silhouette Reader Service
U.S.: 3010 Walden Ave., P.O. Box 1325, Buffalo, NY 14269
Canadian: P.O. Box 609, Fort Erie, Ont. L2A 5X3

The Daddy Salute

MAUREEN CHILD

Published by Silhouette Books
America's Publisher of Contemporary Romance

To my editor, Karen Taylor Richman, with thanks for
her support and her belief in me. Karen, I wish you joy
with your little miracle. You're entering an amazing
new world…enjoy the magic.

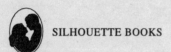 SILHOUETTE BOOKS

ISBN 0-373-76275-5

THE DADDY SALUTE

Copyright © 2000 by Maureen Child

Visit us at www.romance.net

Printed in U.S.A.

Books by Maureen Child

Silhouette Desire

Have Bride, Need Groom #1059
The Surprise Christmas Bride #1112
Maternity Bride #1138
The Littlest Marine #1167
The Non-Commissioned Baby #1174
The Oldest Living Married Virgin #1180
Colonel Daddy #1211
Mom in Waiting #1234
Marine under the Mistletoe #1258
The Daddy Salute #1275

*Bachelor Battalion

MAUREEN CHILD

was born and raised in Southern California and is the only person she knows who longs for an occasional change of season. She is delighted to be writing for Silhouette Books and is especially excited to be a part of the Desire line.

An avid reader, Maureen looks forward to those rare rainy California days when she can curl up and sink into a good book. Or two. When she isn't busy writing, she and her husband of twenty-five years like to travel, leaving their two grown children in charge of the neurotic golden retriever who is the *real* head of the household. Maureen is also an award-winning historical writer under the names Kathleen Kane and Ann Carberry.

IT'S OUR 20th ANNIVERSARY!
We'll be celebrating all year, continuing with these fabulous titles, on sale in February 2000.

Special Edition

#1303 Man...Mercenary...Monarch
Joan Elliott Pickart

#1304 Dr. Mom and the Millionaire
Christine Flynn

#1305 Who's That Baby?
Diana Whitney

#1306 Cattleman's Courtship
Lois Faye Dyer

#1307 The Marriage Basket
Sharon De Vita

#1308 Falling for an Older Man
Trisha Alexander

Intimate Moments

#985 The Wildes of Wyoming—Chance
Ruth Langan

#986 Wild Ways
Naomi Horton

#987 Mistaken Identity
Merline Lovelace

#988 Family on the Run
Margaret Watson

#989 On Dangerous Ground
Maggie Price

#990 Catch Me If You Can
Nina Bruhns

Romance

#1426 Waiting for the Wedding
Carla Cassidy

#1427 Bringing Up Babies
Susan Meier

#1428 The Family Diamond
Moyra Tarling

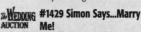
#1429 Simon Says...Marry Me!
Myrna Mackenzie

#1430 The Double Heart Ranch
Leanna Wilson

#1431 If the Ring Fits...
Melissa McClone

Desire

#1273 A Bride for Jackson Powers
Dixie Browning

#1274 Sheikh's Temptation
Alexandra Sellers

#1275 The Daddy Salute
Maureen Child

#1276 Husband for Keeps
Kate Little

#1277 The Magnificent M.D.
Carol Grace

#1278 Jesse Hawk: Brave Father
Sheri WhiteFeather

One

"**Y**ou can't die! Not now." Kathy Tate turned the key one last time, listened to the dreaded coughing and droning of the engine, then shut it off and slapped the steering wheel. "For Pete's sake," she reminded her trusty Bug, "you just had a checkup." An overhaul, she thought with disgust, that had cost her a whopping six hundred dollars.

The battered old VW sat silent, apparently having nothing to say in its own defense.

Well, perfect. She stared out the windshield at the tree-lined suburban street. How was she supposed to get into town and deliver the stack of résumés she'd been up all night typing and printing?

"U.S. Marines to the rescue, ma'am." A deep voice

interrupted her thoughts, and she slowly turned to look out the driver's side window.

Oh, man. Talk about from the frying pan into the fire.

Her heartbeat did a weird little thump as she stared into the crystal-blue eyes of her across-the-hall neighbor, Sergeant Brian Haley. He and a friend of his had been playing basketball in the driveway when she'd left her apartment only a few minutes ago. She'd managed to get past them with just a quick wave, but now she was trapped. By her own blasted car. The traitor.

Her ''rescuer'' bent at the waist, put both hands on his knees and peered in at her. Sharply chiseled features, short, marine-regulation haircut and bare, tanned, sweat-dampened muscles that looked to have been meticulously carved into his chest made for one impressive package. Unfortunately, in the month since he'd moved in, she'd learned that he was all too aware of his impact on women.

Oh, not that he seemed conceited or anything. It was more subtle than that. When he smiled that crooked smile of his, it was clear that he fully expected a woman to turn into a puddle of goo. And, since Kathy Tate puddled for no man, she'd become something of a challenge to him. Lately it seemed that whenever she turned around, there he was.

''Need some help, ma'am?'' another deep voice spoke up, and Kathy swiveled her head to look out the passenger window at Brian's friend. Judging by the high-and-tight haircut, he was also a marine. But then, in Bayside, a town only a mile or so from Camp

Pendleton, you couldn't swing a broom without hitting a marine.

"No, thanks," she said. She didn't need help. What she needed was for her stupid car to start.

"Kathy Tate," Brian said, "this is First Sergeant Jack Harris. Jack, meet Kathy. My new neighbor."

"Hi." He gave her a friendly smile that Kathy returned with ease once she noted the gold wedding ring on his left hand.

"Nice to meet you," she said.

"I say she needs help, Jack." Brian shook his head slowly as he gave the little car a good once-over. Then, looking past her at his friend, he asked, "What do you say?"

"Oh, definitely."

Kathy turned to stare at Brian. One corner of his mouth was tilted into that patented lady-killer smile, but his eyes were all innocence. Yeah. Like she believed *he* was an innocent. "Okay, guys, I appreciate the offer. But look, the car will be okay. It just needs a rest, that's all."

"A rest?" Brian repeated with a short laugh. "For how many years?"

She drummed her fingers on the steering wheel and gritted her teeth. It was one thing for *her* to insult poor old Charlie the VW; it was quite another for somebody else to take a shot at it. "Sergeant Haley…"

"Gunnery Sergeant," he corrected for her.

"Whatever," she snapped, and shot him a look that should have singed the soles of his feet. However, he seemed completely unaffected. "I didn't ask to be rescued, so why don't you just go back to your game?"

He grinned at her and glanced at his friend. "Well, Jack, do the marines wait around to be *asked* or do we go where angels fear to tread?"

"Ooh-rah!" the other man said in a hoarse grunt.

"Oh, brother…"

"From the Halls of Montezuma…" Brian intoned in a deep, steely voice.

"…to the shores of Evans Avenue," Jack finished for him as they both straightened up.

"Come on, you guys," she said loudly, but they were already moving toward the back of her car. Kathy slapped her forehead against the steering wheel once, muttered a curse she hoped her car understood, then hopped out to keep an eye on the cavalry.

They had the little hood open by the time she got there. With their backs to her, she had quite a view of what looked like miles of tanned, muscled flesh. If nothing else, she had to give it to the corps. When they advertised "building men," they weren't kidding.

"So," Jack asked, "what do you think the problem is?"

"Nothing a good round of mortar fire couldn't fix."

"A mortar?" Kathy repeated, leaning over them, trying to keep an eye on what they were doing.

Brian glanced at her over his shoulder and explained. "It's a gun. A really *big* gun."

"Very funny," she retorted.

"Who's kidding?" he asked on a snort of laughter. "This thing's on its last legs."

"VWs can go forever," she said.

"And this one obviously has." He shook his head, reached past a cluster of greasy wires to the shadowy interior of the engine and pushed and poked around for a minute or two. "Still," he whispered, more to himself than anyone else, "never let it be said that a marine couldn't get a machine to run."

"Oh, perish the thought," she muttered. Kathy thought she heard Jack chuckle, but she couldn't be sure. A moment later, Brian stood up abruptly and almost knocked her over. He reached for her automatically to steady her, and where their hands touched, she felt a blast of white-hot heat that nearly swamped her.

He let her go instantly and took a step back, as if he'd experienced that strange sensation, too, and wasn't sure what to do about it. Heck, Kathy knew what she was going to do. *Ignore* it.

"Okay," Brian said, as Jack stood up. "Kathy, get in the driver's seat, and when I tell you, try to start it."

"Fine," she said, knowing it was pointless to try to reason with a man who was attempting to outsmart a car. Besides, it would get her out of his immediate presence and put a nice, solid car door between them.

Once she was settled, she pushed the clutch in, grasped the key and waited for the signal. That's when she heard it—a stream of harsh, guttural sounds pouring out of Brian Haley's mouth. He shouted, he snarled and he did it all in a language she'd never heard before, though she suspected its origins.

Then he called out, "Okay, try it now!"

She did, whispering a little prayer as she turned the key. Instantly good old Charlie fired up, his throaty roar splintering the otherwise quiet of the afternoon.

Both men strolled up to the driver's side window, and Kathy turned to look up at them.

"Outstanding," Jack said.

"Consider yourself rescued," Brian told her.

Okay, so she hadn't wanted their help. She hadn't wanted to be indebted to Sergeant Smile. But it had turned out all right. The least she could do was be gracious. Looking right at him, she squinted into the sunlight and said, "Thanks."

One brown eyebrow lifted, and he nodded his head briefly. "You're welcome."

Then, because she couldn't stand not knowing, she heard herself ask, "Were you speaking in German a minute ago?"

That grin of his widened, and she had to take a firm grip on her blood pressure.

Shrugging, he said, "I was stationed in Germany a few years ago. Learned enough curse words to give any German car a taste of home and shock it into doing what it's supposed to do."

"Why am I not surprised?" she wondered aloud.

"Lady," Brian said as he leaned one hand on the roof of her car and lowered his head to within inches of hers, "as you get to know me, you'll find I'm just one surprise after another."

Kathy smiled sweetly at him and said, "I don't like surprises, Sergeant."

"Gunnery Sergeant."

"Whatever." Then she shoved the car into first, gunned the motor and took off, letting the gunnery sergeant scramble to find his footing.

As the VW coughed and snarled its way down the street, Brian shook his head slowly. "That woman is really starting to get to me."

"Yeah?" Jack said and slapped him on the back. "From where I'm standing, it looks like Hands-on Haley is striking out."

Brian shot him a look and grinned. "Jack, my man, I'm just comin' up to bat."

"Not a chance. That was a clean swing and a miss. I call that strike one." Laughing, he started back toward the driveway to finish their interrupted basketball game.

Brian stared in the direction the VW had gone, long after it had disappeared from sight. Strike one, huh? Well, he had two more coming to him. And he'd never been a man to give up easily.

"Hi, neighbor."

Caught. Kathy stopped short at the sound of that deep, rumbling voice. She'd hoped to get into her apartment without seeing him again today. But apparently the man had some sort of radar where women were concerned. She took a long, steadying breath before turning around to face the man standing behind her.

It didn't help.

As always, her pulse skittered and her heart pounded against her rib cage. Her palms went damp and her mouth went dry.

Brian Haley, six foot two inches of solid muscle and practiced charm stood in the open doorway of his apartment and smiled down at her. And it was truly an amazing smile. Kathy was forced to remind herself, *again,* that she wasn't interested.

Unfortunately, that fact was getting harder and harder to remember.

"Been shopping?" he asked, leaning against the doorjamb and folding his arms across his broad chest, now covered in a red T-shirt emblazoned with the U.S. Marine Corps emblem.

She flipped her hair back out of her face, forced a smile and said, "Boy, nothing gets past you, does it?" Then she hitched the twin grocery sacks in her arms a bit higher.

His grin only widened at the sarcasm. Reaching for the bags, he cradled them both in one brawny arm and said, "Marines are trained observers."

"Lucky me," she said, and took a moment to stick her key in the lock and turn it. Then she made a grab for her grocery bags. "Thanks for the help, but I'll take them from here."

"No trouble," he said, moving out of reach. "Any more downstairs?"

Stubborn, that's what he was. Stubborn and gorgeous and, like all good-looking men, programmed to flirt with any female in range. Well, she'd been flirted with before and withstood temptation. With her less-than-stellar track record in the romance department, resistance was the best defense.

"Your car give you any more trouble?" he asked.

"Nope," she said. "Started up every time all afternoon."

"Probably needs a tune-up, anyway," he told her.

"It just had one, thanks." She opened the door and walked inside, determined not to stand around in a too-narrow hallway with a man whose touch had the ability to start small electrical fires in her bloodstream.

Brian followed her in, still carrying the groceries. She'd let him inside, thank him for his help and then send him the heck out of there, fast.

He set the bags down on the bar counter separating the kitchen from the living room, then turned slowly to admire her place. It looked like her, he told himself. Soft, feminine. White lace curtains at the front windows splintered the afternoon sunshine into frothy patterns that lay across the wood floors in snowflake patterns. Overstuffed chairs and a love seat were pulled up to a round coffee table strewn with books and magazines. Pictures of country lanes and lighthouses dotted the walls, and the faint, sweet scent of lavender flavored the air.

"It's nice," he said after a long moment, and turned to look at her. Her soft brown hair fell straight to her shoulders, then curved under at the ends. A few wispy bangs feathered her forehead and her liquid chocolate eyes looked at him warily. Irritation fluttered through him. He still saw disinterest and a cool distance in her eyes every time she looked at him. After a month of living in such close quarters, you'd think she'd at least let her guard down a little.

Hell, he was a marine.

One of the good guys. Though he doubted that meant a thing to her.

He hid a smile as he realised she was standing in her kitchen, barricaded behind the counter. As far from him as she could possibly get.

"Thanks," she said quietly. "Look, I appreciate the help, but I—"

"You're busy," he finished for her. "I know." He wasn't surprised she was giving him the bum's rush. Though she was always polite, she'd made it clear she didn't want to get to know him as well as he'd like to know her.

And maybe that was a good thing. He didn't like complications. And starting up an affair with a woman who lived right across the hall from him would definitely be complicated.

Then again, he thought with another quick look up and down her small, but curvy body, she just might be worth it.

She cleared her throat, and he blinked.

"Thank you…?" she said pointedly. "And goodbye…?"

"Right," Brian said, nodding. But before he left, there was one thing he wanted to know. Moving a bit closer, he leaned both elbows on the faux butcher-block countertop, locked his gaze with hers and asked, "What exactly is it you don't like about me?"

She looked startled by the question. Sliding her hands into the back pockets of her tight, faded jeans, she cocked her head to one side and said, "I never said I didn't like you."

"You didn't have to," he assured her.

She took a deep breath and sighed it out. "I don't even *know* you."

He gave her a small smile. "We could fix that."

"No, thanks." A quick shake of her head emphasized that statement.

"See what I mean?"

She frowned at him. "Now I've got a question for you, Sergeant Haley."

"Gunnery Sergeant," he corrected her.

"Whatever."

"Shoot."

Both of her eyebrows lifted, and she pursed her lips as if she was actually considering doing just that. A look like that could give a man pause.

After a long moment she asked, "Why are you trying so hard to make me like you?"

"I'm not trying to—"

"You replaced the fixture in the hallway," she said, interrupting his futile attempts to deny her accusation.

Brian had to defend that one. "The landlord wasn't going to do it anytime soon, and that hallway was like the black hole of Calcutta at night."

"Uh-huh," she said, and pulled her hands free of her pockets only to fold her arms across her chest. One foot started tapping against the kitchen floor.

He glanced at it, shrugged and said, "I guess I'm just a small-town kind of guy. Helpful, neighborly."

She smirked at him. "You told me you were from Chicago."

"My neighborhood was small."

She shook her head in exasperation. "You fixed my doorbell without being asked."

"Faulty wiring can cause a fire." He smiled again. No response. So shoot him for being a nice guy.

"Heck, you even washed my car yesterday."

"It was no trouble. I was washing mine, and yours looked as though it could use a bath." Actually, in his opinion her dented, ancient, VW Bug looked as if it needed burying, but now didn't seem the time to say so.

"That's not the point."

"What is the point, Kathy?" he asked, straightening up from the counter and looking down into brown eyes that had haunted more than a few of his dreams lately. "We're the only two renters in this building younger than sixty. Why can't we be sociable?"

She ignored the latter question and answered the former with a question of her own. "The point is, I don't get it," she snapped. "I've made it fairly obvious that I'm not interested, but you keep trying. Why?"

He'd asked himself that question often in the past four weeks, and he'd yet to come up with an answer. So instead of admitting that, he asked a question of his own.

"Is there any reason we can't be friends?"

She smiled and shook her head. "Boy, you're stubborn."

"Marines don't surrender without a fight."

"There's always a first time."

"You haven't know many marines, have you?" he asked.

"You're my first."

Now, he liked the sound of *that*.

Before he could say so, though, she stepped past him, and their arms brushed. Another lightninglike flash of heat shot through him, just as it had earlier today. She felt it, too. He saw it in her eyes, heard it in her soft intake of breath.

He reached out and laid one hand on her forearm. The heat sizzled between them until she took his hand and lifted it off.

Looking into her eyes, he whispered, "There's something between us, Kathy. You feel it, too."

"The only thing between us is that hallway."

"Pretending it isn't there won't make it go away."

"Wanna bet?" she quipped, then walked to the open front door and stood beside it, clearly waiting for him to leave.

Ah, well, he thought. He headed for the doorway. As he stepped into the hall separating their apartments, he turned and laid one hand flat on the door before she could shut him out.

"I'm curious about something," he said, letting his gaze slide over her features.

"What's that?" She stood half-behind the door, using it as a shield.

"Is it all men you don't trust?" he asked, and waited a beat before adding, "Or is it just me?"

One dark-brown eyebrow lifted slightly as she said, "It's *all* men, Sergeant Haley..."

Well, good, he thought.

Then she added, "And especially you."

Swell.

"I'm a very trustworthy guy," he argued.

"And I should take your word for that, I suppose."

"You could call my mother," he offered with a grin.

Her lips twitched, but she shook her head. "Thanks. I'll pass. Now, good night."

Kathy closed the door and instinctively turned the lock. The *snick* it made as it clicked into place seemed overly loud to her in the sudden stillness. Then, going up on her toes, she put one eye to the peephole.

Brian backed up and stared right at her, as if he knew she was watching him. Winking, he said just loudly enough to be heard, "If you change your mind, my mom's number is 555-7230."

Two

The phone rang as soon as Brian entered his apartment. His mind still focusing on Kathy Tate, he crossed the room and absently noticed that the vertical blinds on the front windows were opened. Sunlight speared between the slats, laying prisonlike bars of pale-golden light across the floor. He shook that thought off, snatched up the receiver and said, "Hello?"

"Hi, Bri," a throaty, female voice purred into his ear.

"Dana." He tried not to wince. Even his mother hadn't called him "Bri" since he was eight years old. But, he reminded himself firmly, he hadn't objected to the nickname when he first started dating Dana Cavanaugh.

"I was wondering," she went on, snapping Brian's attention back where she wanted it, "if you'd like to come have dinner at my place tonight."

He glanced over his shoulder at the closed door that led to the hallway, and beyond that to Kathy's apartment. "Dinner?" he asked in an obvious-to-anyone-but-Dana stall. Idly he drew his fingertips through the layer of dust covering the small tabletop. Man, if he couldn't bring himself to clean, he ought to hire someone to do it.

"C'mon Bri," Dana implored and his eyelid twitched in response to the whine in her voice. "It's been *weeks* since I've seen you."

"Yeah, well." A splinter of guilt poked at him. "I've been busy. Work's piling up on base..." That sounded lame even to him. But what should he do? Admit to her that ever since meeting his new neighbor, he'd lost interest in the other women he knew? Hardly. The fact was almost too humiliating to admit to himself.

"Are you too busy to eat dinner now?" she asked.

He shifted slightly to take a look at his kitchen—a small, dark room where no pot bubbled on the stove. Across the hall, Kathy Tate was busy ignoring him, and soon he'd be contemplating which frozen entrée to zap in the microwave. So why was he even hesitating? A dinner invitation should sound to him like a gift from the gods.

After all, it wasn't as if he was making any headway with Kathy. And why shouldn't he have a nice dinner with a gorgeous woman rather than sit here alone regretting the fact that his legendary charm hadn't succeeded in breaching Kathy's defenses? Besides, he hadn't gone anywhere but to the base in the past four weeks.

"Bri," Dana asked, "are you still there?"

"Yeah," he said, "I'm here." Then before he could change his mind, he added, "And soon to be there."

"Really?"

"Why not?" He forced a smile. "What are we having?"

She laughed, and the throaty sound that used to kick his hormones into high gear now seemed forced and just a bit theatrical.

"Let me surprise you," she said.

All kinds of invitations were included in that one sentence, and it really irritated the hell out of him that he wasn't filled with expectation. Was this some sort of weird cosmic justice? Was the perpetual ladies' man destined to lose his heart to the one female who didn't want it?

But even as he entertained that notion, he discarded it. Hearts were not involved here. And if, a few weeks later, he would look back on this moment and wonder how he could have been so stupid…well, he was blissfully in the dark now.

"I'll be there in half an hour," he said, and hung up. A quick shower and he'd be on his way. And hopefully an evening with the delectable Dana would push Kathy Tate out of his mind.

* * *

Fifteen minutes later, Kathy heard his door slam and braced herself for the sound of a brisk knock at her own door. Brian Haley apparently didn't want to take "No, thanks" for an answer.

But his footsteps went off down the hall.

"Well," she said aloud, and was glad there was no one to hear her, "that should teach you a little humility." Without even thinking about it, Kathy walked across her apartment to look out the front windows.

Turning back the edge of the curtains with her fingertips, she looked down onto the residential street below. A group of kids riding their bikes in the late summer sun raced along the quiet street and disappeared, leaving echoed hoots of laughter in their wake. An ocean breeze rattled the leaves of the old poplar trees lining the sidewalks, and somewhere in the distance a lawn mower growled and dogs barked.

She stiffened when Brian hurried down the front steps and along the curving walkway. Following him with her gaze, Kathy didn't miss his crisply ironed blue sport shirt and the tan khaki slacks. Looked like date clothes to her. "I'm glad to see rejection doesn't keep him down for long." She shook her head and went up on her toes to see him better. He moved quickly, like a man on a mission. "Anxious, isn't he?" she muttered through gritted teeth.

So much for her theories about her own irresistibility. Not only wasn't he pining from her lack of interest, he'd gone directly from flirting shamelessly with her to a date with someone else.

Unlocking the door of his black Jeep, he slid inside, fired the engine and was gone a moment or two later.

Only then did Kathy notice her grip tightened on the curtains, pressing dozens of wrinkles into the sheer fabric. She smoothed them out as best she could, then turned around to face her empty apartment.

This was a vindication, of sorts. She'd known all along that Brian Haley was what her mother would have called a womanizer. So she'd done the right thing in standing firm against his flirting and turning down his less-than-subtle invitations to get to know him better.

"I win," she mumbled, and tried not to wonder why victory tasted so much like defeat.

Three days later Brian looked up from his computer screen as First Sergeant Jack Harris walked into the office. "You're late," he said.

"Shoot me," Jack told him, and crossed the room to his own desk.

"Trust me. Today, you shouldn't tempt me."

"Oh, aye, aye, Gunnery Sergeant Haley, sir."

Brian shook his head. "Shut up."

Jack laughed shortly, flipped on his computer and glanced at his friend. "What's the matter with you?"

Brian scrubbed his hands over his face and mumbled. "Nothing."

"Good," Jack said. "I need to see those finished fitness reports today."

"Thanks for the concern," Brian said, "but I'll be fine."

Jack laughed shortly, leaned back in his chair and said, "All right, let's have it."

"Have what?" He bit the words off.

"Could this be..." Jack said, his expression mirroring his amusement, "dare I think it...lady troubles?"

"Who said anything about a woman?" he grumbled from behind his hands.

"You didn't have to," Jack told him. "I recognize the signs."

"What signs?" He dropped his hands to his desk and glared at the other man.

"Signs that a man's been lying awake at night thinking about a woman he can't have."

Brian had been around in the early days of Jack's marriage to Colonel Candello's daughter, Donna. And he remembered vividly how on edge Jack had been then. He also recalled not having had a lot of sympathy for the man. Ironic.

Still, this situation was entirely different. Brian wasn't married. Hell, he hadn't even had a date with the woman slowly driving him nuts. Irritation swelled inside him, and he shot his old friend a dirty look. Pushing away from the desk, he folded his arms across his chest, glared at Jack and demanded, "Why do you automatically assume that I'm having a problem with a woman?"

Jack turned away from his work and grinned. "Maybe because I saw the way you looked at Kathy Tate...and the way she avoided looking at you."

"Thanks for nothing."

"No problem." Jack was enjoying this, and it showed. "So tell me. I saw strike one for myself. Was there a strike two in the past few days?"

"Why in hell did a nice woman like Donna marry you?"

"She refused to settle for less than the best."

"And yet she picked you."

"You're stalling," Jack said, pointing a finger at him. "Afraid to admit you've finally found a woman you can't charm?"

"You're a laugh riot, Jack." Disgusted, Brian snatched up the first of the fitness reports and made a great show of reading it over.

"This is no laughing matter," Jack said soberly and Brian shot him a look in time to see the smile on the man's face. "There's a pool, you know."

"A pool?"

"Yep." Jack rocked easily in his chair, folded his hands atop his chest and studied the water-marked ceiling. "And the pot's getting bigger every day."

"You guys are betting on me striking out with Kathy?" Brian threw a glance at the open doorway and the hall beyond. How many of his "friends" were in on this, anyway? And how, he wondered, sliding a suspicious look at Jack, had they found out about Kathy?

Jack chuckled gleefully. "There's not a marine on base who wouldn't like to see you strike out completely for once."

"Surrounded by friends and supporters."

"Hey, anybody with the kind of luck you have with females is bound to inspire a little…"

"Envy?" Brian provided, one eyebrow arching high on his forehead.

"I was thinking more along the lines of enmity."

"And you felt it was your responsibility to tell everybody about my next-door neighbor."

"After what I saw the other day," Jack said on a laugh, "you bet."

"What happened to *semper fi?*" Brian asked, throwing his hands up in the air. "Marines sticking together? Always faithful?"

"In battle, sure. In this kind of situation, it's every man for himself."

Brian laughed and shook his head. Typical.

"So, what's happening anyway?"

"Nothing," he said on a snort of derision. "That's the problem." Dinner with Dana had been a disaster. As soon as he'd arrived, she'd poured him a drink, told him dinner wouldn't be ready for another hour and suggested several ways to pass the time until then.

Bound and determined to prove to himself—if no one else—that nothing in his life had changed, Brian had given her suggestions his best shot. But in the middle of what should have been a delicious kiss, he found himself imagining that the woman in his arms was shorter, a little plumper, with softly waving brown hair and eyes wide and deep enough to lose himself in.

In short, even Dana's charms couldn't keep his mind from straying to Kathy. Which irritated the hell out of him...and Dana, when he suddenly announced that he'd made a mistake and couldn't stay. With the slam of her door still ringing in his ears, Brian had driven straight back to the base. It was a sad thing indeed to have to admit that work sounded like a better idea than dinner with Dana.

Jack laughed and Brian realized he'd never noticed what an evil chuckle his friend had.

"What's so damn funny?" he demanded.

"It's always entertaining to watch the mighty take a fall."

"A fall?"

"This could be better than I'd hoped," Jack said, amazement in his eyes. "This could work into *love,* Gunnery Sergeant. You may have finally met your match."

Love?

"I think marriage has warped what was left of your mind, Jack. I hardly know this woman..." Then, to make his point, he admitted the most humiliating fact of all. "She won't even go out with me."

"This just gets better and better," Jack chortled.

"Thanks for your support," Brian snapped and jumped to his feet. His uniform boots beat a heavy tattoo against the linoleum floor as he paced back and forth. Then he stopped in front of Jack's desk, shoved his hands into his pockets and said, "I'm not in love, and I sure as hell don't plan to be."

"None of us do," Jack pointed out.

"Yeah? Well, *some* of us," Brian told him, slapping himself on the chest, "have a little more self-control than others."

"Oh, yeah. I can see that."

Brian scowled at him. "Is there a reason why we have to share an office?"

"Probably."

"It's not good enough, whatever it is."

"Hell, Brian," Jack said on another suspiciously evil laugh, "you'll live through this. We all do."

"Quit lumping me in with you and your kind."

"My kind?"

"You know, married marines. Formerly happy men, now dragging wife and family from base to base...packing dishes and furniture and worrying about schools and doctors and God knows what else."

Jack shifted uneasily in his chair and deliberately looked away from the picture of Donna and their daughter, Angela, that had a prominent spot on his desk. "You don't know what you're talking about."

"Sure I do," Brian snapped. "Heck, there's some kind of marriage epidemic sweeping the base. More marines have been picked off here lately than at Iwo Jima!"

Jack stood up slowly, planted both hands on his desk and leaned in. "I wasn't 'picked off,' Brian."

"Sure you were...hell, Donna's a sharpshooter! You never even saw it coming." He lifted one hand to stop Jack from interrupting. "I like Donna, and Angela's the prettiest baby I ever saw, but, man...you were taken out by a sniper and didn't even know it until after the vows were read."

"Back off, Brian."

"No, *you* back off." Nose to nose now, the two men squared off. "You're not sucking me down into the hole you jumped into. I *like* my life," Brian went on, his voice getting louder with every word. "I like packing a duffel and taking off. I like being deployed all over the world. I like living in furnished apartments. I like answering to no one but me."

When Brian finished, he took a deep breath and listened to the sudden silence in the small room. Jack's features were stiff, but after a few seconds ticked away, he seemed to relax a bit. Finally he spoke up. "Who're you trying to convince here? Me? Or you?"

"I don't need convincing," Brian muttered, turning for his desk and the pile of weapons reports that awaited him. "I just needed reminding. So *thanks.*"

"Anytime, gunny," Jack muttered, sitting down and getting back to work. "Anytime at all."

Case closed, Brian thought and felt sanity pour back into his soul. No more moaning around like some lovesick kid. He was a *marine,* for pity's sake. In charge of enough weapons to start World War III. And damn it, it was time he started acting like it again.

He had more names and numbers in his address book than any man he'd ever known. He'd just call a few and get back into the game. He must have been nuts spending the past four weeks daydreaming about a woman who couldn't see him for dust.

Kathy Tate wasn't interested. So what? There were plenty of other women in this city. Mind racing, resolutions forming and solidifying in his brain, he snatched at the phone on his desk when it rang and answered impatiently, "Gunnery Sergeant Haley."

The voice on the other end of the line started talking. With every word spoken, Brian's newly reinforced world started shaking. He couldn't seem to draw air into his straining lungs. His thoughts spun, and his stomach lurched. The familiar sights and sounds around him seemed to evaporate, and all he could hear was the stranger on the phone shattering what was left of his once-so-comfortable life.

Three

"**S**he's getting married again." She cringed inwardly as she said those words aloud.

"Who?" Tina Baker asked.

Kathy shot a long look at her friend, swallowed down the embarrassment choking her and said, "Three guesses."

Tina wiped oatmeal off her infant son's cheeks and frowned thoughtfully. A moment later comprehension dawned on her features. "Your mom?"

Sitting back in her chair, Kathy turned her coffee cup between her hands and glanced at her friend. "Yep. The queen of matrimonial nightmares is at it again."

"Wow." Tina handed the baby a teething ring to

slam against the tray of the high chair, then sat down opposite Kathy. "So this will make husband number five? Or six?"

She made it sound like such a reasonable question. Thank heaven for Tina. Friends since high school, they'd always kept in touch. And no matter how humiliating Kathy found her mother's behavior, Tina had never made a big deal out of it.

Moving to Bayside two years ago was the best thing Kathy had ever done. At least she had one stable person in her life. Tina was madly in love with her husband and constantly trying to convince Kathy that marriage was a good thing.

But Kathy had made up her mind years ago. With her mother, Spring, as a shining example of how not to live your life, Kathy had decided to stay single. Better to live alone than to go from one broken marriage to another.

Not that *that* had ever bothered her mother.

Oh, boy. Wasn't the rule of families that children were supposed to embarrass parents? No doubt, across the country, middle-aged parents were going about their perfectly normal, rut-filled lives, lamenting their offspring's loony life-styles. But not in the Tate family. No sirree.

Nope. Here in never-never land, Kathy was the adult, and her mother was the forty-eight-year-old teenager. Not that she didn't love her mom, but honestly, was it too much to hope for that Spring Hastings-Watts-Tate-Grimaldi-Grimaldi-Hennesey-Butler-soon-to-be would grow up? That she would settle down into the kind of everyday, ordinary mom Kathy had always wanted?

A voice inside whispered, *Yes. She's never going to change, so just learn how to deal with it.*

"Kathy?" Tina spoke up, and Kathy shook her head to clear it.

After taking a quick gulp of coffee, she answered, "Technically, this is marriage number six. But Mom says five. Because she married number three twice, she only counts him as one husband."

Tina smiled, noticed Kathy's disgusted expression and said, "I'm sorry, hon. I know it's not funny, but you've got to admit, your mom is really something."

"Oh, she's something, all right." Kathy shook her head and stood up.

"I swear, her life is like a soap opera."

"Well, I wish she'd hire some new writers."

No matter how kind or understanding Tina was, she'd never really be able to know what it was like growing up with a mother like Spring. Kathy had had to learn early on that she was the responsible one in the household. She'd grown up fast in order to make up for her mom's not growing up at all.

But even as those thoughts rattled around inside her mind, Kathy felt disloyal. After all, her mom had done the best she could. At least she had stuck around, which was more than Kathy's father had ever done.

"So when's the wedding?"

Kathy started wandering around the cozy, cluttered kitchen. Her gaze drifted from the crayon artwork proudly displayed on the refrigerator to the dog bowl on the floor to the child-size fingerprints on the windows. This is what a kid's world should be like, she told herself. And that's why she'd never have children of her own. A bubble of emptiness rose up inside her, then settled down into the pit she usually kept it in. As much as she would love to have the kind of family Tina had, she knew it wasn't in her cards. She refused to be a single mother. She'd seen firsthand just how difficult that was. And she would *never* get married, so that left kids out entirely.

Thank heaven she at least had Tina's kids to pour all of her maternal feelings into.

"Kath?" Tina's voice prompted her. "The wedding? When is it?"

The wedding. "Three weeks," she said, and leaned against the counter.

"She's been single so long," Tina mused, "I wonder what made her decide to get married again."

"Who knows?" Kathy said, throwing her hands high. It had been six years since her mom's last divorce. Kathy had actually begun to hope that Spring was slowing down. Oh, well.

"Where is it?"

This time Kathy had to chuckle. Really, what else could she do with a mom like Spring. "Where else? Vegas."

"Well," Tina said, and reached over to lift Michael out of his high chair, "maybe this time it will work out. Maybe this time she's really in love."

Spring *had* sounded different when she'd called to give Kathy the news about the impending wedding.

There'd actually been a little tremor in her voice. As if she was nervous. Though any woman who'd recited the wedding vows as often as Spring had surely shouldn't have anything to be nervous about. No, it was probably just her imagination working overtime. This was simply another wedding for Spring.

"And maybe our little résumé service will put us both on the Fortune Five Hundred list," she said, and winced slightly. She didn't mean to sound bitter, for heaven's sake.

"Stranger things have happened."

"Anything you say, partner," Kathy said, then changed the subject by asking, "Have you got the new ad ready for the newspaper?"

"Yeah, it's in the other room. Hold the baby for a minute?"

"Sure," Kathy said, always eager to get a little baby hugging in. She stepped forward to pluck little Michael out of his mother's arms. Fifteen pounds of warm, cuddly love squirmed against her, and Kathy's heart melted. She ran her palm gently over the top of his head, smoothing down the wispy, fine, blond hair.

Regret roared through her with a vengeance as she realized again that by denying herself marriage, she was denying herself this. A child of her own to love. And the closer she came to thirty, the harder that truth hit her. The phrase *biological clock* had become pretty much a cliché these days, and darned if she couldn't hear hers ticking.

Michael cooed and batted at her shoulders with two small-fisted hands. She caught one of them and rubbed his little fingers with her thumb. "You're a sweetheart, you know it?" she asked, and grinned when he giggled from deep in his throat.

Tina stepped into the kitchen and paused, watching them. "You're good at that, Kath."

Kathy glanced at her. "It's not hard to love a baby."

"Or a man," Tina said.

"Don't start," Kathy told her, shaking her head. Tina's one major flaw was that she insisted on playing matchmaker.

"There's a guy in Ted's office who—"

"Stop right there," Kathy warned her.

"Come on, Kath. There's no reason for you to live like a nun."

"I don't."

"Really?" Tina laid the manila envelope she was carrying down on the counter and crossed her arms over her chest. "And when was the last time you actually spoke to a real, live *man?*"

Think fast. "Three days ago," she blurted.

"Who?" Tina asked.

"My neighbor."

"The marine?" Tina's blue eyes widened in anticipation.

Oh, man, she shouldn't have started this. Perching Michael on her hip, she bounced him up and down.

"Details, Kath. Details."

"He fixed my car for me," she said with a shrug. "Then he helped me with my groceries." And she'd managed to avoid him ever since.

"And..."

"There is no *and*," Kathy told her, and walked across the room to hand over the baby. Then she snatched up the ad copy and tried to make her escape.

"There could be an *and*," Tina said hurriedly.

"I don't want any *and*." She picked up her purse from the table and headed for the back door. Tina's voice stopped her cold in the doorway.

"You're not your mother, Kathy."

She meant well, but that didn't change the facts. "No, but I am her daughter." Glancing over her shoulder at her friend, Kathy added, "We live what we learn, Tina. And I'd be just as bad at marriage as my mother is. I won't do that. Not to me and certainly not to some poor, unsuspecting baby."

Then she slipped out the door before Tina could continue the old argument.

Brian listened to the dial tone for a few long seconds, then held the receiver away from his ear and stared at it as though he half expected it to blow up in his hand.

"Brian?"

He blinked and shot a quick glance at Jack.

"Bad news?" the man asked.

"Bad?" He didn't know if he'd say *bad*. Maybe catastrophic. Horrifying. But bad? He checked his wrist watch. He only had two hours. Nice of them to wait until the last minute to call.

"Hey, man," Jack said, watching him. "What's goin' on?"

"I, uh…" Carefully, gently, Brian set the receiver down in its cradle. "I have to go."

"Go? Go where?"

"The airport."

"Airport?" Jack sounded as confused as Brian felt. But that couldn't be. No one on earth could possibly be as confused as Brian Haley was at that particular moment.

"Why?"

"I'll tell you later," he said. Later. As in, when he was actually able to repeat the words he'd just heard over the phone. Right now he could hardly force himself to think them, let alone say them out loud.

"Jack, I gotta go." He looked at his watch again. Another minute gone. He felt his life ticking away. The world as he'd known it was about to come to an abrupt end, and there was nothing he could do to stop it.

"Damn it, Brian…"

He shook his head and spared his friend a quick glance. "Trust me on this. I *have* to go." He pushed away from his desk, glanced at the unfinished reports and said, "I'll take care of those tomorrow."

"They're due today," Jack told him. Brian looked at him, and some of his desperation must have shown on his face because his friend took one look at him and offered, "Leave 'em. I'll take care of it."

"Thanks," he muttered, and started for the door. He snatched his hat off the coatrack, then settled it firmly on his head.

"Hey!" Jack called out, and Brian stopped. "Is everything all right?"

Rubbing one hand across his face, Brian swallowed heavily and muttered, "Hell, no."

"Call if you need help."

Help? Hell, he was going to need all the help he could get. But it went against the grain to ask for it. He was a marine, for pity's sake. Tough, strong, dependable. He'd stood fast in battle and lived all over the world. It was his job to protect and defend the United States of America against all of her enemies.

How in the hell could he yell help?

He nodded at Jack, muttered, "Thanks," and left. He ran down the hall, stopping only long enough to help a corporal pick up the files Brian had knocked out of his arms. Then he was out the main door into the California sunshine.

Mentally he heard a clock ticking. Softly at first, then louder as the seconds passed. Time was running out. He had just enough time to get home, change his uniform and make it to the airport.

Then all he had to do was wait. Wait for the stranger from Child Services in South Carolina, who would soon be flying in to deliver into Brian's care the thirteen-month-old daughter he hadn't even known existed.

Ooh-rah.

Four

At the airport Brian stalked through the sliding glass doors and spared a quick glance at the life-size, bronze statue of John Wayne as he passed it. It had to be his imagination, but he could have sworn he heard the big man laugh at him.

But then, hell, who wouldn't?

Hunching his shoulders, Brian hurried past The Duke, cast a quick look at the arrivals screen, then made for gate 36. His footsteps echoed hollowly against the tile, and as fast as that tapping sounded, it wasn't as fast as the pounding of his heart.

Good God. A baby? Him?

He ran one hand across his face and tried to gather the thoughts that had been scattered since receiving that brief phone call.

He could still hear the social worker's voice ringing in his ear. *You recall having a relationship with Mariah Sutton?*

Mariah Sutton. Sure, he remembered her. A couple of years ago. In South Carolina. Pretty, warm, fun. Mariah and he had had a mutually satisfying relationship that had lasted a total of six weeks.

But according to the social worker he'd spoken to nearly two hours ago, the memory of their affair was still alive and well and living in the person of one Maegan Sutton-Haley, thirteen months old.

Brian shook his head as his back teeth ground together. He dodged an elderly woman pushing a black suitcase in front of her like a battering ram, then joined the line of people waiting to pass through the security gate.

Mariah'd given the lady his name, but hadn't bothered to tell him about his daughter. What the hell was *that* about? Why hadn't she told him? He rubbed one hand along the back of his neck and moved forward another inch or two. What would he have done if she *had* told him? he wondered. Honestly, he didn't know. He'd like to think he'd have done the right thing, whatever that was these days. But how could he be sure? He couldn't. Now he'd never know what might have been.

But was that really important at the moment? No. What mattered now was the simple fact that Mariah Sutton had died in a car accident, naming him father and guardian of their little girl.

Damn it, he'd never wanted kids.

Even as that thought entered his mind, another chased right behind it. *If you didn't want kids, you shouldn't have been so careless, huh?*

"Afternoon, Sergeant," the man at the security portal said as Brian moved up to take his turn.

He nodded and stepped through.

Naturally the damn thing beeped.

Brian glanced down at his uniform, guessing rightly that the medals on his left shirtfront pocket had set off the alarms. He looked at the security officer. "Want me to take them off?"

The old man smiled and shook his head. "Just step over here a moment."

Brian left the line and held still while the officer ran a hand-held security wand up and down his body. When it came across the medals, it beeped just like its mother ship had. He shrugged apologetically. "Sorry."

"No problem, marine," the man said, then waved him on. "We're used to dealing with the military. You have a good day."

Not much chance of that, Brian thought. "Thanks," he muttered, and hurried on to meet his fate.

Milling around at the back of the crowd, waiting for the plane to unload, Brian studied the happy, excited faces surrounding him. Apparently he was the only person there who wished he was anywhere else. His heart pounded frantically. Stomach churning, he tried reminding himself that he was a marine for Pete's sake, but it wasn't helping.

Good Lord. A daughter.

What was he supposed to do with a little girl? A baby?

Briefly he told himself he should have paid closer attention when his older sisters had started producing grandchildren for his doting mother. But anytime one of those kids had shown up, Brian had beaten a hasty retreat.

This must be some kind of karmic joke.

One of the airline personnel opened the door for the soon-to-be-appearing passengers, and Brian felt his throat close up. Impossible to be covered in a cold sweat *and* feel completely dried out, but there you go. Actually, he thought, trying to be objective about this, he felt just the way he had the first time someone had shot at him.

The first few people straggled up the gangway, juggling bags way too big to be considered carry-ons by anyone. A few happy squeals sounded from the crowd, and as people slowly met their friends and families and drifted off, Brian stood alone. Waiting.

Then she was there.

A woman came toward him, older, a bit gray, with kind eyes and a tired droop to her posture. Over one shoulder she carried a Winnie the Pooh bag and on her right hip was perched a baby girl.

His baby girl.

Maegan Haley.

God help them both.

"Gunnery Sergeant Haley?" the woman asked as she stopped in front of him and swung the bag to the floor.

"Yes, ma'am," he said, unconsciously shifting stance to attention. His gaze flickered to the baby, who stared at him through eyes so much like his own he felt an invisible fist crash into his belly. Well, whatever else had happened, Mariah hadn't lied.

His daughter.

The woman saw his reaction and gave him a soft smile. "I'm Mrs. Norbert, and this...is Maegan."

"Uh, huh."

"If you wouldn't mind showing me some identification?"

She looked as though she was having second thoughts about handing over the baby. He didn't blame her. Still he showed her all the ID he had and she appeared to be satisfied.

"So," she said, "everything seems to be in order."

Real good, Haley, he told himself. Impress the woman with your articulate style.

But she didn't seem to mind that he'd been struck dumb.

"In the bag there are a few diapers, a bottle of apple juice and some teething biscuits."

"Teething biscuits?" Oh, man, he was in deep trouble here.

"Something like a hard cookie."

"Uh-huh." He nodded, and in an effort to sound at least halfway knowledgeable said, "It looks like she's got all her teeth." He knew this because the baby was baring said teeth at him.

"Oh, most of them, yes," the woman said. "but those back teeth are tough little beggars."

Swell.

"Anyway," Mrs. Norbert went on, "you'll have to do some shopping right away, but at least you don't have to worry about formula."

"Formula?"

"Yes." She looked up at him and shook her head slightly. "Maegan drinks regular milk now, and she can eat people food."

Well that worked out well, but then he hadn't planned on feeding her cat chow.

"Although, you might want to go easy on regular food and stockpile some jarred toddler foods."

"Uh-huh." Numb. Completely numb. And the baby didn't look too happy about the situation, either.

"So! If you'll just sign these..." The woman dipped a hand into her large black purse and pulled out a sheaf of legal papers.

Brian took them and stared down at the words, watching as they blurred and fuzzed. He was about to sign his life away, and for some reason his eyes were refusing to focus.

"A pen. Do you have a pen?" she asked.

"No." A bayonet maybe. A gun. But no pen. "No, I don't."

"Never mind, I do," Mrs. Norbert told him, digging into the bowels of that purse again. "Here, you just take the baby and I'll find it."

With that, she plopped Maegan into her daddy's arms, and man and child stared at each other warily. Brian studied her, noting the heart-shaped face, the string of drool hanging from her pouting mouth and the butterfly hair clip attached to impossibly fine, light-brown hair. She wore a frilly blue dress, shiny black shoes and white tights straining over a well-padded behind.

Brian held her exactly as he would a live grenade—with extreme caution, at arm's length.

Maegan looked him over, and he was pretty sure she didn't approve of him. Of course, how could he blame her? Some strange woman had just loaded her onto a plane, flown across the country and dropped her into the arms of another stranger. What did she have to be happy about?

As if to prove him right, Maegan started kicking her little feet wildly, then screwed her face up into a mask of displeasure just before howling like some crazed hound on the scent of fresh meat.

"Geez!" he choked out. "Hey, hey stop that," he told her, and jiggled her slightly.

The only effect that move had was to make the sound of her cries go up and down like a talentless kid playing scales on the piano.

"Oh, pay no attention," Mrs. Norbert said as she came up with the long-sought-for pen. "She's just tired and cranky."

"I know how she feels," he muttered. In fact, he was getting crankier by the minute.

"Excellent," she said, taking the baby from him so he could sign the papers that would make him solely responsible for one tiny, *loud* scrap of humanity. "I'm sure you'll get along wonderfully well. It will just take some time."

Yeah, he thought, as his daughter calmed down and glared at him. About thirty years ought to do it.

But Brian Haley was a man of honor. So he signed those papers, taking custody of the child he'd made, and with every stroke of the pen felt the last of his world crumble.

"Right," Mrs Norbert exclaimed, then tore the top sheet of paper off and tucked it into her purse. Then she gave Maegan a resounding kiss on the cheek, a final squeeze and handed her over to Brian. "Now if you two will excuse me, I've got to run. My sister's flown in from Portland to meet me, and we're going to have a few days holiday at Disneyland."

As the social worker bustled off, Brian's gaze followed her until she was lost in the crowd. "Sure, she's going to Disneyland." He turned then to look into his baby girl's accusatory glare. "And you and I, we're headed for the Black Lagoon."

Kathy leaned in close and put her ear to her front door, straining to hear what was going on in the hallway.

Of course, she could just simply open her door and ask Brian Haley what the heck he was up to. But, as she kept reminding herself, she was avoiding the man.

Still, he wasn't making it easy on her. For the past couple of hours, she'd heard him coming and going and the sounds of heavy items being dragged along the hall. She peered out of the peephole, but even with the light he'd fixed, she couldn't see much. Just his open apartment door and the broad expanse of his back as he carried something into the apartment. Then he shut his door and even that view was lost to her.

She came down off her tiptoes and frowned to herself. What in the heck was he up to, anyway? But the moment that thought shot through her mind, she reminded herself she didn't care. Brian Haley was no business of hers.

But her hand strayed to the spot on her arm where he'd touched her a few days ago. It was almost as if she could still feel the heat of his flesh on hers.

"Ridiculous," she muttered, and determinedly walked away from her front door toward the desk she'd been sidestepping all day. Time to get to work. Those résumés weren't going to type themselves. But the minute she sat down, she thought she heard something.

Cocking her head, she listened again, then when the sound came, she stood up and moved to the front window. Opening it, she stuck her head out and craned her neck, looking for the source of that tiny wail.

But there was nothing.

With twilight deepening, the street was nearly deserted, her neighbors no doubt seated around their dinner tables. A soft summer breeze slipped into the room, ruffling the papers stacked on her desk. Automatically she reached over and set a small, rose quartz crystal atop the pile to hold them in place.

Shaking her head, she turned away from the window, telling herself that she was imagining things. There was no baby crying. Her building held four apartments. On the ground floor there was Mrs. Cassidy in one and Mrs. Steinberg in the other. Both ladies were well into their sixties and neither one of them had grandchildren come to visit, as they would be happy to tell you with any encouragement at all. Upstairs there was only her and Brian Haley. Since she didn't have a baby and the very notion of Brian with one was laughable, Kathy decided she'd either imagined that cry or she was experiencing hallucinations due to a severe caffeine deprivation. Opting for the latter explanation, she headed for the kitchen and her coffeepot.

"Give me a break, kid," Brian pleaded, jiggling the baby on his hip as he held the phone to his ear and waited for his mother's monologue to wind down.

Mary Haley, while surprised and delighted to find out she was a grandma again, had had several dozen things to say to her son on the subject of fatherhood.

Maegan sniffed, rubbed both eyes with her fists and shook her head until the butterfly clip went sailing off her hair.

"Should have left you with Jack and Donna a while longer," he muttered as he started swaying. Somewhere in the back of his mind he remembered one of his nephews being calmed by the whole swinging motion. He hoped to hell it would work on Maegan, too.

"What do you mean?" his mother demanded. "Leave her with whom? For how long?"

He rolled his eyes. "Friends. A couple of hours." He closed his eyes against the memory of Jack's shocked face when he'd seen Brian Haley with a baby.

No doubt there'd be lots of questions coming from that quarter really soon. But thankfully, Donna had taken one look at Brian's frantic expression and had cut her husband off at the knees when he'd started an interrogation. Knowing Jack, Donna's maneuver was only a delaying tactic.

Taking a deep breath, Brian reminded himself to stay calm. It wouldn't do him a damn bit of good to irritate his mother—the one woman he'd been sure would be willing to help him out. The woman lived for her grandchildren and adored babies. "I had to go to the store. Got enough stuff to outfit the Third Battalion. Didn't want to drag her through the shopping."

Didn't want to put himself through it, really, but it amounted to the same thing, didn't it?

"So you left that poor baby with *more* strangers?" his mother demanded.

"She didn't seem to mind," he said. In fact, the little girl had seemed more than willing to be out of her daddy's presence. Maybe babies could smell fear.

"So what's she like, my new granddaughter?" his mother asked.

As Maegan opened her mouth to howl again, Brian sighed and said, "She has great tonsils."

"So I hear," Mary Haley said on a laugh.

"Look, Ma," he said, speaking loudly enough to be heard over the din of his daughter, "you've got to help me, here. I'll pay your ticket out. Stay a couple of days…weeks." *Years,* he thought helplessly.

"No can do, sweetie," she said and didn't sound the least bit sorry, damn it.

"What do you mean?"

"I *mean,* I raised my babies. Now it's your turn."

Raise her? Hell, he was just trying to find a way to survive the night.

"Honey," his mother said, "you'll do fine."

"I don't know what I'm doing."

"And whose fault is that?" his mother asked. "If you'd come home for visits more often, you'd have been around your nieces and nephews enough to learn a few things."

Exactly why he'd stayed away, he wanted to say, but he restrained himself.

"It won't be easy, Brian," she said, "but you can do this. She's just a baby. She *needs* you."

That hit him hard.

Maegan quieted, sniffed again, then laid her head down on his shoulder. A stab of something warm and completely foreign sliced through him, right down to his bones.

She *did* need him.

This tiny little girl needed him to be brave and strong and *sure.* He owed her that. Hell, he owed her mother that. No one had ever really needed him before. Not the way she did. Completely. Her survival, her future, depended solely on him.

"Brian?"

"Yeah," he said, and cleared his throat to get rid of the gruffness in his voice. "I'm here."

"Look, honey, I'd like to help you, but I'm going on a cruise the end of this week."

"A cruise?" he repeated, though he did vaguely

remember her mentioning a trip the last time he'd spoken to her.

"Yes. You remember? A sight-seeing cruise to Alaska? I'm going with that nice Edith Turner? You remember her? Her daughter was the one with the big wart on her forehead?"

His chin hit his chest. Typical. Edith Turner's daughter had grown up to be a district attorney and yet she would always be "the girl with the wart on her forehead."

"Yeah, I remember."

She must have been able to hear the weariness in his voice, because a moment later her tone softened and she said, "Brian, honey, you've been given a great gift."

His gift drooled all over his uniform shirt.

"I know it seems scary right now—"

"I never said I was scared," he protested.

"Of course not," his mother agreed. "But if you were a little nervous about this, it would be understandable."

Okay, *nervous* he could admit to without feeling like a wimp.

"I suppose." Maegan was asleep, and Brian was afraid to move for fear of waking her and setting her off again.

"I've always thought you'd be a wonderful father, Brian," his mom said, surprising him. "And this little girl will be your ticket into a fabulous world."

Remembering the social worker, he muttered, "Yeah. Disneyland."

"Oh, better, honey," his mother promised him. "Much better." Then briskly she said, "As soon as you get leave, you fly home and show me my grand-daughter, all right? Good night."

"Sure, Mom," he said. "Bye."

When he hung up, he had the oddest sensation of having cut off his last lifeline to the outside world. Now it was just him and a baby girl who hated him.

Five

His responsibility.

Hell, he knew that. And he wasn't a man to shirk his duty, either, he thought, gently easing the baby into a more comfortable position on his shoulder. All he'd wanted was a little help. A sort of *guide* to walk him through the minefield of motherhood. And, Brian thought with a pang of something he refused to identify, a little sympathy wouldn't have been out of line.

At that thought his heart twisted and he winced at the feeling.

"Yeah, right," he muttered. Like he deserved the sympathy? If he thought *he* was having a bad day, what about Maegan? She'd lost her mother and then been flown across the country and tossed into the arms of a big man she'd never seen before. If anyone deserved sympathy around here, it had to be her. "Poor kid," he whispered, and blew the wisps of her hair out of his face before they made him sneeze. "It's not your fault you got stuck with me, is it?"

She sniffled in her sleep and shifted her head around restlessly.

Instantly he stiffened as if he'd been shot. Hell, if she woke up, he'd be in real trouble. His gaze swept the apartment, noting the boxes of baby stuff and the unpacked bags of groceries. Packages of disposable diapers, for God's sake, were piled high on his coffee table, and there were enough jars of baby food spilled across his kitchen counter to open a day care nursery.

He had to put all that stuff away somewhere, then he had to assemble the baby's bed and somehow, some way, decide what to do with her tomorrow while he was on base, and yet he couldn't do any of that because if he moved, she'd wake up and start screeching again.

Mentally he took a long, slow count to ten, hoping for some kind of control. Some kind of miraculous wisdom to float down from the cosmos and infiltrate his fried brain.

Nothing.

His glance fell on the phone again. There had to be someone he could call for—not help, he told himself—*advice.* Dana? Brian shook his head. Nope. He was pretty sure she wasn't speaking to him. Besides, Dana, like all the other women he'd ever dated, would be even more lost around a baby than he was.

He'd never been drawn to the home-and-hearth type of female until, of course, he'd moved in across the hall from Kathy.

"Kathy!" In his relief he nearly shouted her name and instantly paid the price for it.

Startled into wakefulness, Maegan pushed away from his chest, opened that sweet mouth of hers and bellowed as loud as any general he'd ever heard.

"Oh, man..." Bouncing her up and down in his arms, Brian tried reasoning with her. "C'mon, kiddo," he said as he patted one big hand against her back gently. "Crying leads to wrinkles, didn't you hear?"

She frowned at him, took a deep breath and let out another howl.

"Okay, so you're not worried about your looks yet," he said, swaying wildly from side to side. "How about, if you stop crying, I'll buy you a car when you turn sixteen?"

Her little fists curled into his uniform shirt and somehow managed to grab hold of a few chest hairs to boot. When she yanked, he wanted to howl right along with her.

"All right, so you're too young to be bribed." He eased her fists open and sighed at the relief. Then, looking into her tear-streaked face and red-rimmed blue eyes, he said, "You realize you're leaving me with no choice."

She didn't seem to care.

Helplessness rolled around inside him and he didn't like it one damned bit. He'd spent his entire adult life ordering others around. He wasn't a man to stand back and wring his hands. Glancing down into those tear-filled eyes, though, Brian knew he was beaten. At least for tonight he needed help. And though it went against the grain to have to crawl to the woman who'd been so pointedly ignoring him for weeks, he really didn't have much choice.

"Okay—Kathy it is," he muttered, and headed for the door. "I only hope she'll take pity on you, if not me."

Kathy was already moving toward her door, drawn by an infant's cries, when she heard the frantic knocking.

She threw the door open and came face-to-face with a harried looking Brian Haley, cradling a furious baby girl.

"What on earth?"

"Look," he said quickly, and stuck one foot in front of her open door as if afraid she'd slam it shut on him. "I didn't want to bother you, but, lady, I am out of options."

The sergeant? Don Juan Haley himself? With a baby?

What next? Space aliens landing in her front yard?

The baby's cry broke into her thoughts, and she looked up at Brian before asking, "Whose…?"

"Long story," he said briefly.

"Later," she told him as briefly, reacting to both the unhappy child and the wild-eyed look in Brian's blue eyes.

It was the first time since he'd moved in that Sergeant Brian Haley had looked anything but in complete control. But she didn't have the luxury of enjoying his frustrated confusion. Her heart ached for the baby crying so miserably, and instinctively Kathy reached for her.

"What's wrong with her?" she asked, stepping back into her apartment as she soothed and whispered to the trembling child. At the moment she didn't care if Brian followed her in or not. All she was interested in was easing the poor baby in her arms.

"I don't know," he said, and stepped in behind her.

Kathy looked over her shoulder at him in time to see him scrape both palms along the sides of his head in an age-old sign of helplessness.

"Every time she's awake, she cries," he said. "I don't know how to stop her."

Frowning, Kathy felt the little girl's bottom, then stared at the man watching her. "You might try changing her diaper," she said. "The poor thing's soaked."

His head fell forward as if he was just too tired to hold it upright any longer. A moment later, though, he lifted his gaze to hers. Shaking his head, he said, "You're right. I didn't even think of that."

For one lightning-brief instant, Kathy felt a stab of pity for the big, gruff marine. Obviously he was completely lost when it came to babies. Her gaze swept over him, and she had to admit that it was the first time she'd seen him when his uniform wasn't in tiptop, picture-perfect condition.

A line of baby drool meandered down the front of

his shirt, and his left forearm, where the baby's wet bottom had been perched, was damp from wrist to elbow. Amazingly enough he hadn't seemed to notice. His tie was crooked, and even the row of medals on his pocket looked slightly askew. And his crystal-blue eyes shone with a quiet desperation that reached her at an elemental level. All in all he was the picture of a man at the end of a very short rope.

All right, so she'd been avoiding him for weeks. So she hadn't wanted to get close to him in any way. It didn't matter now that he was a love-'em-and-leave-'em type, did it? This wasn't about relationships. This was about a baby and an apparently out-of-ideas man.

Should be safe enough.

"Do you have extra diapers?" she asked.

He snorted a laugh. "Does China have tea?"

Kathy followed him out of her apartment, across the hall and into his place. She stopped short on the threshold, staring in stunned amazement at mountains of *stuff*. Well, this explained all of his trips up and down the hall all day.

She gave a look to the still-sniffling, but generally quieter, baby in her arms. Jiggling her gently, she smoothed one hand up and down the little girl's back and whispered, "Boy, you've really turned him inside out, haven't you?"

Brian marched through the mess directly to a pile of diapers. He tore open a package and turned around, holding one diaper in an outstretched hand like a peace offering. The hopeful expression on his face was hard to miss.

"You want me to change her?"

Relief shot across his features. "Would it help if I begged?"

Her lips twitched, but she swallowed the smile before it could grow. Snatching the diaper from him, she walked to his couch, laid the baby down and got to business.

He watched every move she made, and while she worked, she heard him muttering under his breath, though she was only able to understand about every other word.

"Diapers…wet…didn't think…poor kid…hopeless…"

With the wetness off her bottom, the baby seemed much more agreeable, and Kathy lifted her onto her lap, smoothing her little skirt down over chubby knees. A twist of frustrated maternal instincts had her fingers linger on the lacy edge of the girl's hem before she turned to look at the man standing opposite her.

"Thanks," he said tightly, and shoved both hands into his pockets.

"You're welcome."

He nodded. "I suppose you want to hear that long story now.…"

"Oh, yeah," she admitted. She was definitely wondering why a confirmed bachelor, a sergeant in the marine corps, was suddenly buying out baby furniture stores. Where had the little cutie come from?

He nodded again and pulled one hand from his pocket to scrape along the side of his head one more time.

If he kept that up, he'd rub away the little hair the marines let him have.

"Y'know what?" she asked suddenly. "Why don't we take care of the baby first. Get her settled…. She is staying here, right?"

"Yeah," he said tightly.

"Okay, then. When she's down for the night, you can tell your long story."

He looked relieved.

Bouncing the baby slightly, she asked, "Have you fed her?"

"No."

Wet diaper, no food, no wonder the poor little thing had been screaming. Shaking her head, Kathy stood up, perched the baby on her hip and headed for the kitchen, with Brian only a step or two behind her.

"Well, there's no shortage of food," she murmured.

"I got a little of everything," he said, and waved one hand at the dozens of jars scattered across the countertop.

"So I see. How about bottles? Have any of those?"

"Yeah," he said, squeezing past her in the too-tight space, headed for yet another brown bag. As his hips brushed against her backside, Kathy gulped in a breath of air and deliberately tried to ignore the swift, undeniable rush of heat that swamped her. Busy here, she told herself. Baby first, hormones later.

Correction…hormones never.

Brian pulled a bottle from the bag with the flourish of a man who'd stumbled across a gold nugget.

"Great," she told him. "Fill it with milk and warm it a little in the microwave."

"Milk," he repeated, then smacked his own forehead with the flat of his hand. "I didn't buy milk."

"You're kidding? There's something you forgot to buy?"

He leveled an unamused smile at her, and she shook her head.

"I have some in my fridge," she told him.

"Saved." He eased past her again, and Kathy gritted her teeth against the sensation of him rubbing against her.

While he was gone, she sat the baby on the counter, rummaged around in drawers for a spoon, then standing in front of the baby to keep her from falling off, opened a jar of applesauce.

The little girl's mouth opened eagerly for that first bite, and Kathy laughed and kept the food coming. In no time at all the applesauce was gone and the baby's eyes were beginning to droop.

Brian finally came back with a warmed bottle of milk, and Kathy took it and the baby into his bedroom. Laying the girl in the middle of the bed and propping pillows alongside the open edge, she gave her the bottle and watched as the milk quickly began disappearing.

Before the bottle was half-empty, the baby was sound asleep, one hand lying across her still-tear-stained cheek.

Kathy turned her gaze from the child to the room

she'd been sure she would never see. *Spartan* was the first word that came to mind.

A battered chest of drawers, a straight-backed chair with camouflage uniform pants draped across the seat. A pair of boots lay discarded in one corner of the room, and a stack of paperback books towered unsteadily beside the bed. Directly opposite the bed were mirrored-glass, sliding closet doors.

He caught her reflected gaze with his, and even in the dim light through the open door to the living room, she saw trouble in their depths.

With another quick look at the baby, she led the way back to the living room, getting as far away from that king-size bed as she could get.

He moved to close the bedroom door, and Kathy stopped him. "No, leave it open so we can hear her."

"I don't want to wake her up."

"As long as we don't yell, we won't. She's pretty tired."

"Big day," he commented dryly.

"For both of you, I'm guessing," Kathy said, and took a seat on the couch.

He dropped into the closest armchair, propped his elbows on his knees and cradled his head in his hands. "You have no idea," he said, before lifting his gaze to meet hers.

Unbelievable. And humbling, he thought. Kathy had come into his apartment, calmed the baby and brought him peace again…all in less than fifteen minutes. Hell, at the moment she made a better marine than he did.

So the first night of his new life was taken care of. Now all he had to do was figure out the next thirty years or so.

"Try me," Kathy said, reminding him that she was still waiting to hear his "long story."

Sighing, he leaned back in the chair and looked at her. For weeks now he'd been trying to get her into his apartment. Trying to get her alone. Well, here they were. Alone in his apartment…with a sleeping baby twenty feet away. What was that old saying about being careful what you wish for?

"She's my daughter," he blurted out, figuring he might as well get used to saying the words aloud.

"Your daughter?" Her voice lifted on that last word into an eerie realm of disbelief.

He couldn't blame her.

"You sound as surprised as I was a few hours ago when I first heard the news." Although he doubted very much that her heart was racing, her stomach spinning and her brain slipping into something that was just short of a coma.

"You're telling me you didn't know you had a child?"

"That's about it," he said tightly, rubbing one hand across aching eyes. Embarrassing to admit to that little tidbit, he thought. Then, while he was on a roll, he went on and told her the rest of it. About Maegan's mother, their brief affair and her tragic car accident only a week or so before. "In her will she left instructions that Maegan was to be delivered to her father—me."

"What about her family?"

"She didn't have any."

"And that's the first you heard of Maegan?"

Her voice sounded strained, like she was squeezing words past her throat. Well, hell. What did she have to be so annoyed about?

"Yeah. Mariah never said a word to me about a baby."

"So this is all *her* fault?" Kathy asked.

Brian looked at her warily.

"Did you give her a chance to tell you?" she asked.

"A chance?" Hell, they'd spent nearly every night of six weeks together. You'd think she could have found a spare minute or two to impart that knowledge without him taking her aside and saying, Now's a good time to tell me if you're pregnant or not.

"That poor woman," Kathy continued without waiting for an answer and pushed off the couch to pace. "Having a baby alone...and then dying when the child is so young she won't even remember her mother."

He'd thought of that, too, and it broke his heart a little for both Maegan and Mariah. They'd been cheated out of time together.

But he couldn't very well change that, could he? Of course it was sad. And tragic. If Mariah hadn't died, they'd all have been better off.

Kathy shook her head as she walked briskly from one side of the living room to the other and back again. Brian recognized anger when he saw it, but for the life of him he couldn't figure out what he'd done to deserve it.

"What are you so hot about?"

"This is just so...*male,*" she said.

"What?" Man, it was never a good thing when a woman started generalizing about the male gender.

"You guys," she said. "All of you. You roll in and out of relationships. You never stick around. You make promises you don't keep, and inevitably it's the women and children who get hurt."

Pride stung and personal integrity attacked, Brian had to fight back.

"Hold on a minute, lady," he said, and shoved himself up from the chair. Just a foot or two away from her, he looked into her chocolate-brown eyes and continued, "You can't lay this all off on me. What about Mariah? She could have told me about the baby. For whatever reasons, she chose not to."

"What would you have done if she had told you?"

That brought him up short. After a moment's pause he lifted both hands and let them drop again. "Honestly, I don't know. And now I'll never know. Because she didn't give me that choice."

Her full lips tightened just a bit, but she nodded as if agreeing with him.

"As for breaking promises," Brian went on, feeling a rush of outrage fill him as he stared at the woman who looked offended enough for all womankind, "I've never made a promise I didn't keep. I don't know what kind of man you're used to dealing with, but my word means something to me. I don't give it lightly."

Kathy almost believed him. His blue eyes flashed. The stubborn tilt of his square jaw and the tense set of his broad shoulders all went to convince her that maybe she was wrong about this particular man. Maybe.

But what else was she supposed to think? He'd been flirting with her like crazy for weeks and hadn't exactly seemed the home-and-hearth kind of guy.

Still, now he was the father of a baby girl, and by the looks of things he was in way over his head.

"Okay, I'm sorry," she said, more to change the subject than for any real need to apologize.

He nodded.

"Have you thought about what you're going to do with her now that you have her?"

"Hell," he said gruffly, turning from her to walk to the window that overlooked the neighborhood behind them. "I haven't had a chance to think about anything."

"You can't take her to the base with you."

She thought she saw him shudder, but she could have been wrong.

"There's a day care center on base," he said, as if considering it for the first time.

Kathy's stomach jumped.

"But she's in a strange place already. Does she really need more strangers to deal with?" And why was she arguing against a perfectly good solution to the sergeant's problem?

"I suppose not," he agreed stiffly, and rubbed one hand across the back of his neck. "But I don't know what else to do. In case you hadn't noticed," he added with a wave of his hand at the room around them, "I'm a little out of my depth."

"I could watch her for you while you're at work. At least temporarily, I mean, until things calm down around here and you decide what you want to do." The words were out of her mouth before she could stop them. She blinked and could almost see those words hanging in a bubble in front of her face, as though she were a character in a comic strip. Quick, she thought. Somebody hand her an eraser.

Too late.

Brian Haley turned toward her and the streetlamp from outside haloed his head and shoulders in a pale, white light. "Are you serious?"

Was she? Kathy thought about it for a second or two. She worked at home. Made her own hours. She could do it. And the memory of little Maegan cuddled against her warmed her right down to her toes. She could pour all of her stifled maternal urges into that one small bundle of humanity who probably needed it just as badly as Kathy did.

The only problem would be in dealing with Brian Haley on a daily basis. Even when she'd been avoiding him, he'd had a serious effect on her. Spending too much time with him could get...difficult. But she was a big girl, not some teenager driven by bouts of lust and fantasies. She could handle it.

"Yeah," she said quietly. "I think I am."

"Why?" he asked just as quietly.

Couldn't blame him for being curious. She'd stone-walled his advances for weeks, and now she was volunteering to put herself in harm's way every day.

"Does it matter?"

He studied her for a long moment, then released a heavy sigh. "At this stage of the game," he mused, "I guess not." A half smile curved his mouth as he took a step toward her.

She shook her head and backed up a step. Better to get some things settled right off the top. "Don't misunderstand, Sergeant. I'm going to take care of the baby. Not you."

He raised one light-brown eyebrow, and Kathy's toes curled. Oh, brother, what was she letting herself in for?

"Strictly business?" he asked.

She cleared her throat noisily. "Business."

"It's a deal, then," Brian said and held out one hand.

She looked at it as if it was a snake, and had to work up her nerve before she slid her hand into his. But even braced for the contact with his skin, as his fingers curled around hers, she felt a white-hot burst of light shoot straight from her fingertips along her arm to dazzle her heart.

"Deal," she repeated, forcing her voice to work despite the knot lodged in her throat. Then she pulled her hand free, but couldn't stop the tingling sensation burning just beneath her flesh.

She could feel it in her bones.

She was in deep trouble.

Six

The first week of Brian's new life made boot camp seem like a vacation in Tahiti.

It wasn't hard enough, trying to get a little sleep while being kept awake listening to every snort and sound the baby made for fear she'd stop breathing in the night. Oh, no, he had to put up with Jack Harris's constant stream of questions and survive a mountain of unsolicited advice on parenting from a man who only two years ago was as blissfully ignorant on the subject as Brian himself.

He was being sucked into a world he'd never wanted to enter. He was learning things he had no interest in knowing and doing things he would have laughed at if someone had prophesied it a month ago.

Add to all that the fact that every time he turned around, Kathy was taking him shopping for more baby stuff and you had one unhappy marine.

Who knew kids needed so much junk? How had any child ever been raised properly without an electric dirty-diaper container or a baby monitor or a deluxe stroller with optional extra seat, he wondered? And who in the heck had come up with the item he'd just seen? Flushable potty targets! Thank God he had a girl, not a boy—he wouldn't have to teach her to aim.

Pitiful, what his life had come to.

Brian groaned quietly and let his gaze scan across the latest baby department he'd found himself in. Two aisles over, Kathy had Maegan perched on one hip as she flipped through rows of dresses, pj's, sweaters, shirts and shorts. His eyes glazed over. What difference did it make how many clothes a baby had? It's not as though she was going to wear them out playing ball or something. Although, he reminded himself with a sigh, she did manage to dirty up every shirt *he* owned.

Who would have thought such a pretty lady could contain so many disgusting fluids?

"Excuse me," a woman's voice said from close by, and Brian turned to look at the middle-aged salesclerk hovering at his elbow.

"Yes, ma'am?"

She smiled and shifted her gaze toward Kathy. "I believe your wife's trying to get your attention."

The word *wife* had him stiffening up instantly. But he looked at Kathy and nodded as she waved him over. He walked toward her, his gaze scanning her thoroughly from head to toe. Oh, there were lots of words he could use to describe Kathy Tate. But by his definition *wife* wasn't one of them.

This forced togetherness was getting harder and harder to handle. Every morning, baby in tow, he was at her door at 0430 hours. And every morning she was wearing a short, blue nightgown that barely covered the tops of her thighs. He knew this because the silk robe she habitually wore over it was usually hanging open, giving him a too-excellent view of her physical charms.

Which were plenty.

And every afternoon when he arrived to pick up the baby, Kathy greeted him smiling. Invariably there was some delicious aroma wafting from her kitchen, and she looked pretty damned appetizing herself in her always-present jeans and T-shirt.

Oh, she was helping him all right. Helping him toward an early heart attack.

"Hold the baby for a minute," Kathy said as he came close and she handed Maegan over.

Briefly, father and daughter stared into each other's eyes, and Brian looked for signs that the kid was getting used to him. But he was pretty sure he still detected a faintly wary gleam in those blue eyes of hers. Still, he held her propped against his shoulder and ignored the drooly fist that clutched at his hair.

"Are we about finished?" he asked, and told himself that wasn't a whine in his voice. Marines didn't whine.

"Yeah," Kathy said, giving him a quick look. "Just one or two more things and that's it."

He waited while she grabbed up a white sweater, then followed her to the checkout stand where he dug into his wallet and reached for his credit card that was still steaming from its last use. The clerk snatched it from him as if he would change his mind if given a chance and began to ring up the purchases.

"Where to next, General?" Brian asked.

Kathy looked up at him, reaching out a hand to brush Maegan's hair back from her little face and said, "Actually, I think that about does it."

"You're kidding," he said, feeling relief stampede through him.

"Nope. Maegan's pretty well fixed, I'd say."

"Sign here, please," the clerk said, and held out a pen.

Kathy took the baby. Brian signed the bill, trying not to look at the total, then took his receipt and shoved it into his jeans pocket. He picked up the bag and turned to the women in his life. "So where to?" he asked. "How about dinner?"

Tempting, Kathy thought. All too tempting. For a week she'd been moving further and further into Brian Haley's life. Seeing him every morning and every afternoon had already become a habit for her. A habit she was beginning to enjoy far too much.

Damn it, she should have known better. She'd offered to help him mainly because Maegan had slipped into her heart almost from the first moment she'd seen her. But over the past few days, Kathy'd begun to realize that it wasn't only the baby she had feelings for. In idle moments her brain always drifted to thoughts of Brian Haley. Her dreams were filled with images of his big, broad hands moving over her body, his fingers dipping inside her, teasing her into a maelstrom of sensations. And every time, she woke dazed, warm and just a little more unsatisfied than when she'd fallen asleep.

She watched him learning to be a father, and her heart twisted a bit each time she saw the big man cradling the tiny child they now shared. There was something so touching, so vulnerable about a big man unafraid to be gentle, she thought, and caught herself. Good heavens, this was getting completely out of hand. She had to pull back. Had to get a comfortable distance between them again. Before it was too late.

"Kathy?" he said, and waved one hand in front of her face. "Dinner?"

Dinner. Sure, they'd start with dinner, then there'd be "dessert," then before she knew what had hit her, breakfast.

"Uh—" she stalled briefly "—no."

"No?"

Why did he look so blasted surprised? Did he really expect her to be able to drop her whole life for him? Did he think she had nothing more important to do than to spend time with him and Maegan? Well, of course he did, she told herself. She'd been doing just that for the past week, hadn't she?

"No," she said again, making it a bit firmer this time. "I...already have plans."

"Oh."

She looked up into those big blue eyes of his and felt her resistance melting. Instinctively she locked her knees, lifted her chin and handed him the baby. Much easier to resist him when she wasn't holding such a little cuddler. "Thanks for asking, though."

"Sure. No problem," he said, but didn't sound convincing. "C'mon, I'll take you home."

So where was she? Brian wondered for the fiftieth time that night. Crossing quietly to the front door, he opened it, stuck his head out, looked down the hall. No sign of her.

He checked his watch. Nearly midnight. Not so late, he told himself, then wondered again where she was and who she was with.

Scowling, he drew back inside and closed the door. None of his business, he thought, if she didn't care enough to make her date pick her up at her door. Hell, she'd taken off four hours ago to meet the guy somewhere. She should have told him where, he thought now, worrying a bit. What if the guy was a psycho? What if he kidnapped her or something? What if he was a lousy driver and wrapped the car around a telephone pole?

And what if, he told himself sternly, he stopped going off the deep end?

He didn't really think she was in danger. What was bugging him was much more basic than that. What had him crawling the walls was knowing that some guy was touching her, holding her, damn it…probably kissing her. If not worse.

Whoops. Don't go there, marine, he told himself. He wasn't about to start imagining Kathy stretched out naked atop somebody else's bed.

He wanted that image of her in *his* bed. Where it belonged.

Damn it.

"Thanks for going to the movies with me, Tina," Kathy said as she drove her friend home.

"Hey, it was a treat," the other woman said with a laugh. "Anything that gets me out of the house for a few hours is a good thing."

"Yeah, it was fun," Kathy said, and wondered if Brian had had any trouble getting Maegan to sleep.

"So how's the baby?" Tina asked as if she could read her friend's mind, and something in her tone had Kathy sliding her a glance.

"What's that supposed to mean?" She stopped at a red light and turned to look at the woman's too-innocent expression.

"Nothing…" Tina shrugged her shoulders, glanced at her fingernails then said. "I just wondered how you were getting along with Sergeant Sensational and the Wonder Baby."

"Sergeant Sensational?"

"You forget," Tina said, sighing dramatically. "I've seen him. And, boy, if my Ted wasn't such a cutie, I'd be tempted."

Kathy laughed aloud. Tina was nuts about her husband, and everyone knew it. "Fine, you let Ted go and I'll snap him up."

"Changing the subject," Tina said, wagging her index finger. "We're talking about your marine, not my insurance salesman."

"He's not my marine."

"Not yet, anyway."

The light changed, and Kathy gratefully returned her attention to the dark street ahead of them. Still, she protested. "I'm just helping him out for a while."

"Uh-huh."

"Look, he's new to this whole baby thing. It's only neighborly."

"Uh-huh."

Kathy's back teeth ground together. She'd never really noticed how infuriating Tina could be. "There's nothing going on between Sergeant Haley and me."

"More's the pity."

"Tina, you know how I feel about—"

"I know, I know," Tina interrupted. "Love sucks, and marriages don't last."

Stung, Kathy bit her bottom lip and stared hard at the road.

"I have plenty of reasons for feeling like that," she finally said.

"I'm sorry, Kath," Tina whispered, "but honestly, hon, don't you ever wonder what it would be like to throw caution to the wind and take a chance?"

No, she didn't. At least, not often. And when she did, she talked herself out of the notion quickly enough.

"Thanks, but I've seen my mom take enough chances for all of us," Kathy said.

"And how miserable is she?" Tina asked quietly.

Miserable? Spring was about as far from miserable as Mary Poppins was from Attila the Hun.

Still— "That's really not the point."

"What is the point, then?" Tina shook her head, half turned in her seat and stared at Kathy's profile. "Living your life alone, like some vestal virgin tucked away on a mountainside just so no one can stay long enough to walk away?"

"Wow," Kathy muttered, feeling that solid hit shake her to the core. "You've been storing that up for a while."

"I guess so," Tina muttered, apologetic again. "We've known each other too long to pull punches, right?"

"Right," she said, though she was still reeling a little from Tina's last assault.

"Okay, then. I worry about you."

"You don't have to."

"That's one of the perks of caring for someone," Tina told her. "You're alone too much, Kath. You should find a nice guy and take a chance on love. Heck, you've got a perfectly good marine going to waste right across the hall from you. Live a little. You might be surprised at what you get."

As Kathy pulled her car to a stop in front of Tina's house, she put it in park and turned to look at her closest friend. Even in the dim light she could see what it had cost Tina to speak up, and Kathy loved her for it. Even though she disagreed.

Oh, she was more than tempted by Brian Haley. And that was why she couldn't afford to relax her guard. If she did allow herself to care for him, then she'd only be devastated when he eventually left. And he would leave.

"I appreciate it, Tina. I really do. But I know just what I'd get. A soggy pillow from too many tears. There are no surprises, Tina. Ask my mom."

Brian threw his door open when he heard her footsteps in the hall.

Kathy jumped, startled when he stepped out into her path. Hand on her pounding heart, she stared up at him and said, "What's wrong? Is the baby all right?"

"The baby's fine," he said tightly.

Relief, sharp and strong, swept through her. "Then what is it? What are you doing?"

His eyes widened and he shook his head as if he couldn't believe she even had to ask what the problem was.

"Do you know what time it is?" he asked in a voice that could only be described as a growl.

If his features weren't as dark as a thundercloud, she might almost find this funny. She hadn't had someone waiting up for her since she was fifteen. Then she forgot about the humor in the situation as she noticed his broad, bare chest. The silver dog tags hanging from around his neck glinted in the hall light and shone brightly against his tanned skin. The jeans he wore weren't completely buttoned up, as if he'd thrown them on in a hurry. Her breath caught as she noted the paler skin in the open vee of the buttons and realized he wasn't wearing anything under those jeans.

Oh, my.

Kathy drew her gaze up, across that amazing chest of his and up to icy-blue eyes that bored into hers. Trying for a lighthearted tone despite the thundering of her own heartbeat, she said, "Gee, Dad, sorry I'm late."

Those long legs of his moved fast, and in one smooth step he was right next to her, only inches from her, in fact. She felt the heat of his body reach out for her, and there was suddenly nothing she wanted more than to move in close, rest her head on his chest and feel his arms wind around her. Licking dry lips, she told herself to get a grip, even as his hands closed on her upper arms and tugged her a little closer.

"Believe me, baby," he said in an iron-clad voice, "I'm not feeling fatherly."

Oh, she could see that, she thought with a nervous hiccup that must have sounded like a laugh.

"It's not funny," he ground out. "I was worried."

He had been. She could see it in his eyes, feel it in the tension in his hands. It was a new and not totally unpleasant sensation, having someone—okay, a *man*— worry about her. But she had to remember to keep her distance. Brian Haley wasn't in her future, so it would be dangerous to allow him into her present.

"You didn't have to," she said quietly, and wondered why her voice sounded so breathy.

"Couldn't help it," he told her, his gaze moving over her face with a slow, caressing appreciation.

She wouldn't have thought it possible, but her heartbeat actually sped up even further. Amazing, the effect he had on her. Heat snaked up from his hands and along her shoulders and down her spine to pool at the backs of her knees. Wobbly. He actually made her weak in the knees.

"Your date couldn't even bother to see you to your door?" he demanded, and looked past her down the hall as if he expected to see a cowardly shadow slinking away.

Her "date" was probably already tucked into bed beside her husband, but she couldn't very well tell him that. So instead she said, "I don't need to be escorted inside. I can take care of myself. Have for years."

Finally a small smile curved one corner of his mouth. "I'll bet you have. But the way I see it a man takes his woman to the door, sees that she's safe before leaving her."

Oh, my.

She swallowed heavily. By rights, her streak of feminism should be standing up and screeching. But somehow his words made her feel not inferior but cherished. And she wondered how it must be to have that feeling all the time. To know that a man cared enough to put your safety, your concerns, first.

His fingers moved on her arms, massaging her flesh through the sheer material of her red silk blouse.

Every one of his fingertips seemed alight with flame. She felt his touch down in the deepest, darkest corners of her soul. As if a single match had been set to dry kindling, a tiny flame was springing to life inside her, and if she didn't do something soon to stop it, it would blossom into a bonfire that would consume her entirely.

"I..." She paused to clear her throat. "I have to go inside now."

He nodded slowly, as if he heard her but was in no big hurry to comply. "I'll see you to your door."

She lifted one limp hand and pointed at the door, not two feet away. "It's right there."

He took one long step backward and drew her with him, never letting her go.

"I really should be going inside." Why didn't she sound more sure about that?

"I know," he said, and let her go long enough for her to dig in her purse for her key. Then he took it from her, unlocked the door and opened it wide, glancing into the lamplit interior of her apartment before turning back to look at her again. "Now I know you're home safe."

"Am I?" she asked, knowing she was talking about something far more dangerous than physical safety. It was her heart that was in danger here.

His hands slid up her arms, over her shoulders, along her neck. Kathy shivered at the feel of his strong fingers against her flesh, and as he cupped her face in his wide palms she held her breath, not sure what she was wishing for.

"You're as safe as you want to be, Kathy Tate,"
he whispered, just before he lowered his head to slant
his mouth across hers.

She braced for it. Knew that the first touch of his
lips would be a soul-shaking experience. And even
then, knowing what was coming, she trembled in his
grasp.

His hands framed her face, his thumbs smoothed
across her cheekbones, and his lips, his mouth, did
wonderful things that she hadn't dared dream about.
Softly at first, he kissed her thoroughly, barely caressing her mouth with his. She rose up on her toes
and leaned into him, hoping for more, wanting...
needing more.

And then, with a deep groan from the back of his
throat, he gave her all that she demanded. His fingers
slid back along her scalp, threading themselves
through her hair. He pulled her closer, tighter against
him, and she wrapped her arms around his middle
hoping to find purchase in a suddenly rocking world.

His tongue parted her lips and slid into her warmth,
and she gasped at the first taste of him. His breath
invaded her and became her own. His tongue danced
with hers, twisting, twining, exploring. His teeth
tugged at her bottom lip, sending jagged shards of
sensation splintering through her bloodstream.

Breathless, her mind spinning, her heart reeling,
Kathy tried to hold on to her sanity, but instead felt
those fragile threads slip from her grasp. And when
he finally broke the kiss and looked down into her

eyes, she read more passion than she'd ever known before written on his strained features.

Letting her go suddenly, Brian took a hasty step back toward his own front door. Scraping one hand along the side of his head, he muttered thickly, "Now you had better go inside."

"Yeah," she whispered, though she knew it was far too late for her to try for safety. She stepped through the door and started to close it when she noticed him still standing there, watching her. "What?"

He shook his head and gave her a small smile. "I'm waiting until you're inside with your door locked."

"Still taking care of me?" she whispered.

"I'm trying, baby," he said, "but it's not easy."

She knew he meant that it hadn't been easy to stop what they'd been doing. She could see for herself that his breathing was every bit as ragged as hers. And the bulge in his jeans was graphic proof that by taking care of her, he was letting himself in for a long, frustrated night.

"You keep looking at me like that," he muttered, and she lifted her gaze to meet his, "and we'll be taking care of each other all night."

Her stomach pitched and she felt herself go hot and damp at the thought. But she determinedly gathered the threads of her sanity and nodded before closing the door and turning the lock.

Inside she leaned back against the door and closed her eyes. She'd been wrong about what she'd said to Tina.

Apparently, there were *plenty* of surprises.

Seven

"**Y**ou *lost* them?" Brian bellowed into the face of a private who looked as though he was ready to dig a hole and climb into it.

"Yes, Gunnery Sergeant," he said, snapping to attention.

Fuming, Brian looked away from the kid for a moment, hoping to get a grip on his rapidly rising temper. His gaze snaked across the open, brushy, beach land that surrounded Camp Pendleton. Rolling hills, dusted with the fading glow of the sun, jeeps and tanks dotted the landscape, with marines hovering near their machinery like anxious parents. Seagulls swooped down from the sky, looking for any discarded tidbit of food as they dodged helicopter blades thwapping the air with a rhythmic pulse.

Day over. Time to wrap everything up and head for home. And this idiot kid loses a pair of night-vision goggles.

Slowly he swiveled his head back to glare at the fool in question. "Private," he said in a tight, low growl, "the U.S. Government *loaned* you those goggles. The U.S. Marine Corps *trusted* you to have enough sense to hold on to them."

The kid stiffened further and a muscle in his jaw began to twitch.

Brian leaned in close until he was looking eyeball to eyeball with the impossibly young marine. Geez… was he really getting that much older, or were the recruiting officers going to junior high these days? Nose to nose, he went on in a snarl, "Those goggles cost more than you did, boy."

"Yes, Sergeant."

"And you're gonna find 'em."

"I am, Sergeant?"

"Do you expect *me* to find 'em for you?"

"No, Sergeant," he said quickly, and swallowed hard enough to send his Adam's apple bobbing like a cork on a fishing line.

"You think maybe we ought to call your mommy out here to find 'em for you?"

The kid stiffened further. "No, Sergeant."

"Well, good," Brian snapped. If there's one thing his marines had to learn, it was responsibility. He wasn't about to fill out a report stating that one of his kids had lost an expensive piece of equipment. Hell, if he let this go by, the next thing you know, the damn fools would be losing their guns.

These kids had to figure out that they'd better take damn good care of their equipment or one day they might find themselves surrounded by the enemy with only rocks to throw in their own defense.

"Private Henry," he said, his voice a low, dangerous weapon in its own right, "you're gonna be the most popular man in your squad tonight."

The kid blinked.

"Everybody stays right here, combing every inch of this place until we find the goggles *you* lost."

A wave of murmured complaints reached him, but Brian ignored it. Not only would the squad hate Private Henry, but they wouldn't be too damned fond of their sergeant, either. But then, he wasn't in the corps to win popularity contests. Hell, did they think *he* wanted to stay out here all night going up and down marsh hills? He had a life, too. Okay, at the moment it was a pretty confusing life, what with the baby and his reaction to kissing Kathy last week.

But it was his.

"All right, you bunch," he ordered, turning his head until he could spear each of the waiting marines with a glare as cold and sharp as a bayonet. "Get busy. You climb every hill, you slink into every valley. Look behind every damned blade of grass. Pick up every rock, and brush the sand away by hand if you have to, but find those goggles. Nobody leaves until you do."

As the men moved off, giving Private Henry a few

well-chosen insults, Brian stared out at the ocean and the sun about to sink into the horizon. A cold wind swept off the water and surged across the land as though it could plough a road for the waves to follow.

Ordinarily he liked being out here, running exercises. He enjoyed watching a new crop of marines learn to do what the corps had been doing for more than two hundred years…protecting this country and its citizens. He reveled in showing the new guys what they could find in the corps. Duty. Honor. Comradeship. And hell, he always got a kick out of seeing some young devil dog drive a tank into the ocean by mistake.

A half smile dusted across his mouth and was gone again. But today he didn't even find enjoyment in testing out the weapons.

He watched the unceasing line of waves pound against the shore and retreat again. The roar of the ocean rumbled beneath the overlying noise and hustle surrounding him, and he realized that today he didn't even feel the usual sense of satisfaction in being a part of such a community of warriors.

Because today, like every other day for the past week, he was thinking about Kathy Tate and what she was doing to him. For almost two weeks, now, he'd been a father. And though he was beginning to reach a sort of truce with the blue-eyed heartbreaker who'd invaded his life, her baby-sitter was a different story altogether.

He sucked in a gulp of sea-flavored air, jammed his hands on his hips and asked himself why in the hell he was letting her get to him this way. Damn it, no woman had ever come as close as she had. Always before, he'd managed to keep his lady friends in a specific sort of "comfort zone."

Close, but not too close. Intimate, but not really. Lovers, but not *love*. And in that one, unbelievable kiss, Kathy had breached way too many barriers for comfort. If he was a man to whom running came easy, now would be the time to head for the hills.

Thankfully, that line of thought died out quickly when a jeep roared up behind him. As the engine was cut off, Brian turned to watch Jack Harris clamber out of the driver's seat and walk toward him.

"What's goin' on, Brian?" he asked as he turned his gaze to watch the men moving off slowly across the field.

Shaking his head, he replied, "Henry lost a pair of night-vision goggles."

"Oh, perfect." Jack snorted and kicked at the low grasses at his feet.

"Gonna be a long night, if we don't get lucky."

"We don't have that kind of luck."

"No kidding."

"Think I'll call Donna and tell her what's going on," Jack said and pulled a cell phone out of his uniform pocket. "If I don't warn her that her dinner might be ruined, I'm a dead man." He moved off a couple of paces to make his call.

Brian snorted a choked-off laugh at his old friend checking in with the little woman, then acknowledged Donna would have his hide if she ever heard him refer

to her like that. His smile faded completely when he
realized that he had a call of his own to make.

Gone were the days when he answered only to himself. In fact, he could hardly remember a time when
he'd had his apartment...and his life to himself. He
wasn't the free-wheeling gunnery sergeant anymore.
Now there was a baby to consider, not to mention the
woman who was taking care of that baby. And what
if Kathy had a date tonight? He scowled fiercely at
the thought. She'd gone out three times in the past
week, and each time she left, it had driven him to
distraction. He'd tried a couple of times to get a look
at her mystery man, but the guy never walked her to
her door.

Which sure as hell didn't say much for him.

Jack walked up beside him again, and Brian said,
"Can I use your phone?"

Jack's eyebrows went straight up. "What is the
world coming to? Hands-on Haley needs to report
in?"

"Shut up and give me the phone."

Jack held it just out of reach. "Still at strike one,
or has there been another development I haven't heard
about yet?"

Instantly that kiss and the resulting week-long silence ran through Brian's mind, and his expression
must have mirrored his thoughts. Jack's laugh boomed
out over the sound of the helicopters, and a couple of
nearby marines turned to stare. Brian ignored them.
"What's so damned funny?"

"You, man," Jack told him. "Strike two!"

Brian lunged for the phone. "You don't know what you're talking about."

"I gotta see this woman," Jack went on as he gave up the phone. Slapping Brian on the back, he added, "Bring her and the baby over for dinner, huh? Donna wants to look at her, too."

"Surrounded by friends," Brian muttered, and turned his back to the other man. Hell, if he could get her to go out with him, he wouldn't be striking out, now would he?

Then, as if he could read minds, Jack spoke up again. "Or maybe," he mused as Brian dialed, "she's still refusing to go out with you?"

Brian inhaled sharply and muttered a curse that would have started a fight if Jack had heard it.

"That's it," Jack crowed. "Oh, man, the money in the pool is going to really pile up when the guys hear this."

Great. Perfect. His life had turned into the hottest gambling pool on base.

He tuned his "friend" out and listened to Kathy's phone ringing. She picked up on the third ring. "Hello?"

"Kathy, it's me."

"Hi," she said, and he wondered if he was imagining a smile in her voice.

"Look," Brian went on, lifting his gaze to where the squad was just climbing over the first hill in their search. "I've got a problem on base."

"What's up?"

Did she sound worried?

"A private lost some equipment, and I'm keeping them out here until they find it."

"Oh," she said, and this time he knew he heard disappointment in her voice. Had she been looking forward to seeing him at the usual time?

"I was wondering," he went on, "would you mind watching Maegan a few more hours?"

"It's no problem," she said.

He lowered his voice in case Jack was listening. "No *date* tonight?"

"Uh…no. Not tonight."

Brian didn't know if he was relieved that she wasn't seeing the guy or disappointed that she wouldn't have to cancel on the man.

"How late do you think you'll be?"

Hmm. Could be half an hour or two days.

"No telling," he said with a sigh. "Until these ya-hoos find what they lost."

"Boy," she said, "I'm glad you're not my boss."

He was, too, because if she worked for him, he'd be in serious danger of a sexual harassment suit.

"I'll be there as soon as I can," he said, reluctant to hang up and lose the sound of her voice.

"Oh!" She sounded surprised, shocked.

"What?" he demanded and took a step forward, as though he could just leap into her apartment. "What happened? What's wrong?"

"Nothing's wrong," she said quickly, and then in a sweet, singsong voice, added, "Maegan, what a big girl you are."

"What'd she do?" he wanted to know, and suddenly felt light-years away from the cozy apartment and his baby girl.

"She let go of the couch and almost took a step. Oh, Brian, she looks so proud of herself!"

"A step?" He grinned and tried to picture the little girl wobbling back and forth on chubby legs. Briefly he considered how a month ago he couldn't have imagined being so excited over what should be a natural process. But in the next instant he realized that his life was not only different now, but better. "That's great," he said, wishing he was there to share in the triumph. "Give her a kiss for me."

"I will," Kathy said, and her voice dropped huskily.

"And, Kathy," he continued, staring out over the marsh grass.

"Yes?"

What was he going to say? Kiss yourself for me, too? No. Any kissing that was going to be done, he wanted to be in on it personally.

"Nothing," he said softly.

"Oh. Okay, then," Kathy said. "I'll see you... whenever."

"Okay. And thanks."

"You're welcome."

He pushed End and shut the power off. Half turning, he held the phone out to Jack, and when the other man took it without a word, Brian wanted to thank him. He didn't think he was up to any more jokes at the moment.

"Couldn't help overhearing," Jack said.

He should have known the guy couldn't be quiet for long. "Yeah?"

"Maegan's walking?"

Surprised that his comment hadn't been about Kathy, Brian turned around to look at his friend. An understanding smile creased Jack's features, and Brian nodded.

"Almost a whole step," he said, and heard the pride in his voice. Amazing. Three weeks ago, he'd have laughed at anyone who would have told him that he would be a doting father in less than a month.

"Boy, when Angela first took off a couple of months ago," Jack was saying, "I was prouder than three generals."

Brian nodded thoughtfully. He used to smile indulgently while Jack gushed about his gorgeous wife and brilliant daughter, all the while telling himself that Jack didn't even know he was a trapped man.

Now he was practically in the same boat and only just beginning to realize that *trapped* wasn't really the word for it. Who would have guessed that Brian Haley, king of the short-term relationship, would fall so much in love with his daughter and so much in lust with a woman who was unlike any he'd ever dated.

"So," Jack asked, keeping his voice neutral, "getting back to the main subject, was strike two a swing and a miss?"

Scowling, Brian thought about it a moment. That kiss had surely not been a miss. But it hadn't gotten him anywhere but deeper into the frustration that had been clawing at him since moving in across the hall from Kathy. So if the kiss was strike two… Finally, he said, ''Foul ball, high and away.''

Nodding sagely, Jack told him, ''Then all you have to do is straighten it out.''

Brian shook his head in disgust. ''First, I have to get up to bat again.''

''You will,'' Jack said, and turned toward the squad slowly making their way over the marsh hill. ''But first, you have to get off this field and back into the playing field.''

True enough. He wouldn't get anywhere until those blasted goggles were found. Sighing, he led the way across the brush grass. ''Damn privates,'' he muttered.

Jack laughed.

A gentle knock on her door woke Kathy at 2:00 a.m.

Jumping up from the chair where she'd been dozing, she shook her head to clear away sleep-induced cobwebs and hurried to the door. She opened it and looked up into Brian's crystal-blue eyes. He looked exhausted…and entirely too good.

''Sorry it's so late,'' he started to say.

''Don't worry about it,'' Kathy said, cutting him off as she reached for his hand and drew him into the apartment. ''But it's so late now, why don't you just leave Maegan with me for the night? She's sleeping soundly, and it just doesn't make sense to move her.''

He inhaled sharply and blew the air out in a rush. Nodding, he said, ''That's fine. Thanks.''

He scraped one hand across his face, and Kathy felt

for him. She could just imagine wandering around in the darkness for hours on end. "C'mon," she said, and led him into her small kitchen. Pushing him down into one of the two chairs at the tiny table, she said, "Just relax. I'll get you something to eat."

His smile warmed her through and she told herself she was being ridiculous to be so touched by such a small thing.

"Food sounds great," he said, and leaned both elbows on the table to cradle his head in his hands.

While she bustled around the kitchen, she asked questions about what he'd been up to and let him talk about his night. By the time she had a sandwich made and a bowl of steaming soup in front of him, his story was winding down.

"Anyway, we found the goggles in a ditch the idiot had been sitting in." He shook his head. "For some reason he set them down, then just walked off without them when the squad was called in."

Kathy took the seat opposite him. "I'll bet he won't be doing that again anytime soon."

"Lord, I hope not." He tucked into the rich tomato soup, and in seconds the bowl was empty. "I didn't even realize how hungry I was," he said as he started on the sandwich.

"Would you like something to drink?" she asked as she picked up his bowl to refill it.

"If you have a beer," Brian said, "I might have to worship you."

She laughed, enjoying the feel of the late-night quiet and the man watching her every move. "Then get ready to hit your knees, Sergeant.'' Opening the fridge, she pulled out a can of beer and carried it and the soup back to the table.

''A man could get used to this, oh goddess of all things good and tasty.''

Her toes curled, but she kept her voice light.

''And every woman deserves to be worshipped occasionally.''

He opened the beer, took a long drink and practically purred in pleasure. ''Baby, consider yourself worshipped.''

His voice seemed to scrape along her nerve endings, leaving her insides trembling. While she struggled for breath, she told him, ''Finish your dinner, and I'll go check on Maegan.''

Brian nodded and dug into his second bowl of soup. Logically he knew it was canned, but it tasted like homemade. The sandwich was thick, and the beer went down like fine wine. After the night he'd had, this all seemed too good to be true. Just a month ago, he'd have gone into his empty apartment, collapsed atop his bed and gone to sleep hungry.

Of course, staring across the table at Kathy's sleep-ruffled hair and slumberous eyes, not to mention the pale-blue nightgown she wore, was stirring up a completely different type of hunger. One that had been slowly devouring him from the inside out for more than a month.

Grumbling to himself, he finished his sandwich just as she came back into the room.

''Sleeping like a baby,'' she said with a smile.

"Good," he said, and heard the exhaustion in his voice. God, he felt as though he was nailed to the chair, and he didn't know how he would work up the energy to cross the hall into his own place.

"Come with me," she said quietly, and Brian looked up to see her holding one hand out to him. He took it and let her pull him up, then lead him into the living room where she practically pushed him down onto her overstuffed love-seat sofa. "Now just sit there for a minute and relax."

He smiled at her and noticed how the dim lamplight seemed to cloud around her in a golden haze. Was his vision blurry or did she really seem to shine?

She curled up in the chair across from him, braced one elbow on the arm of the chair and cupped her chin in her palm. "Feeling better?" she asked.

"I might make it," he said as his gaze strayed to where her silk robe parted to give him a lovely view of one of her breasts pushing against the fragile material of her nightgown. His body stirred and his palms itched, but though the spirit was willing, he had a feeling that he was just too tired to get the job done. Even if she'd go for it. Which he doubted.

Shame, really, he told himself tiredly. He had a feeling he and Kathy together would make the fireworks display on the Fourth of July look like a stink bomb. His eyes drifted closed on the thought, and though he fought to hold them open, this was one battle he couldn't win.

Kathy smiled softly as she watched him. It was so hard to define her feelings about this man. Only a month ago she'd been avoiding him like the plague. Now here they were, alone together in the middle of the night, and she was watching him sleep with a fondness she wouldn't have expected.

But it was more than that, she knew. She'd enjoyed waiting up for him. She'd enjoyed making him a meal and watching him devour it in grateful gulps. She'd liked listening to the sound of his voice in the stillness of her apartment.

Brian Haley was turning out to be so much more than she'd thought at first meeting. He wasn't just a smooth-talking marine with a practiced flirting mechanism. He was also kind, thoughtful, gentle and patient with the baby who'd moved into his life and heart. And to top it all off, he was so damned sexy he'd become the starring attraction in her nightly dreams.

It was a mistake to care for him. She knew that. And yet, she couldn't seem to stop herself. His smile, his voice, his touch had already wormed their way into her heart, and she didn't know how to get them out again.

Sighing, she stood up and moved over to the couch. Lifting his legs onto the couch, she put a pillow behind his head and let her fingers smooth back his hair. He slept soundly, probably too exhausted to realize where he was. Picking up the afghan she'd crocheted herself, she flipped it open, then let it fall down atop him, covering him from chin to boots. As she stood there, wondering if she should try to pry those boots off his feet, she felt him take her hand.

Instantly that wild flash of heat jolted her system. Her breath caught, and she wondered if she would ever become used to the effect he had on her.

Kathy looked down at him, but his eyes were still closed. He tugged at her hand, pulling her down beside him. Leave now, she told herself sternly. Go to your room and close the door. But she did neither. Kathy sat uneasily on the edge of the couch, looking at their joined hands. His fingers, his palms were so big, so strong, and yet she'd seen the gentleness in his touch. Warmth from his body seeped into hers, and when his thumb scraped along the back of her hand her heart fluttered uneasily.

Still more asleep than awake, Brian tugged at her again, moving back against the cushions to make room for her.

Danger, her mind warned.

But her heart overruled her head for once, and Kathy stretched out alongside him. He murmured something in his sleep that she didn't quite catch, then pulled her closer, into the circle of his arms.

Holding her breath, Kathy half expected him to make another move. To stroke her, to try to seduce her into the lovemaking they'd both wanted for so long. And a part of her acknowledged that if he did, she probably wouldn't resist this time. But that expected move didn't come, and in another moment or two Kathy accepted what he offered and relaxed against him.

Using his broad chest as a pillow, she listened to the steady sound of his heartbeat beneath her ear. His arms closed around her, and she felt his breath brush against the top of her head. It felt right, somehow, to be with him like this. A baby sleeping in the next room, a soft light shining from the corner and a world of stars just beyond the windowpane.

Somehow this sweet closeness was even more intimate than lovemaking, she thought. Lying there with him, she let go of her worries, her fears and, just this once, let herself be held.

Eight

Soft, pearly light filtered through the lacy curtains at the windows as dawn crept closer. Kathy shifted on the couch, closing her eyes tighter against the growing light. She didn't seem to have much room, and in her half-awake condition, she tried to stretch out.

Her hand smacked Brian's chin, and when he grunted, she rolled backward in surprise. Eyes wide open now, she stared at him as his strong arms came around her in time to keep her on the narrow couch cushions. How could she have forgotten where she'd fallen asleep the night before?

He looked just as surprised to see her, but then his eyes warmed up, and a slow, seductive smile curved his mouth. Sergeant Smile, indeed.

"'Morning," he whispered while his hands stroked smoothly up and down her back.

She knew darn well she should put some distance between them, but at the same time, another voice deep inside her whispered, *Too late now, Kath. You made your bed last night, now you have to lie in it.* And all in all, she didn't mind a bit. At least not now, when his hands seemed to be jump-starting her body into more life than she'd ever had, before that first glorious cup of coffee.

"'Morning," she answered, moving into his caress like a cat trying to direct the strokes of the person petting it.

His right leg rested between her thighs, her breasts pressed against his chest, and she felt a decided tingling sensation in her nipples as he shifted slightly to allow himself a better hold on her.

Good. It felt too good, she told herself as she sighed when one of his hands slipped beneath her pale blue nightgown to caress her bare back. His fingers dusted across her flesh with the lightest of touches, sending small, firefly-size sparks shooting through her bloodstream.

"I've wanted to wake up like this for a long time now," he said, and she heard the raw huskiness in his voice, appreciated it as it slid over her like a warm blanket.

"Brian..." she said, and was never sure later if she had been about to say "Don't" or "Please do." But it didn't matter, because a moment later he pressed his mouth to hers and any chance of turning him away dissolved in the heat.

There was nothing gentle in his kiss. It was pure, unadulterated hunger. As if he'd been starved for weeks, he took her mouth as a hungry man might when offered a banquet. His tongue slid in and out of her warmth with a steady regularity that pulsed within her. She turned her head, slanting her mouth to meet his eagerness with her own.

One hand slid up her back to cup her head and she felt safe, secure in his strong grasp. Kathy clutched at his shoulders and matched his tongue's movements, giving as well as taking, conquering as well as being invaded. He groaned, and she smiled inwardly at the flash of pure, female power that swept through her.

She let her hands slide down from his shoulders to his chest, and even through the fabric of his white T-shirt, she felt the sharply defined muscles she'd so admired in the past. But it wasn't enough. She needed to feel his skin, scrape her short, straight nails along his flesh. She needed to explore every inch of him by touch as much as by sight.

While his mouth tormented her, she slipped her hands beneath his T-shirt, and at the first contact with his bare skin, she felt him shudder against her.

"Baby," he muttered as he pulled his head back to look at her, "you do things to me with a simple touch that I would never have believed were possible."

She inhaled sharply and let her fingers glide up, up his body until they found his flat nipples. Then she stroked them gently with the pads of her fingers, and his arms tightened around her until she thought her ribs might snap.

"That's it," he murmured and flipped them over, lying atop her on the too-narrow couch. He looked down at her and his gaze moved over her so slowly her body warmed in response. Then he lifted the hem of her nightgown and slowly, leisurely, drew it up, exposing her skin to his sight by inches.

Kathy squirmed beneath him, loving the hard, solid feel of his body pressed along hers. But when she reached up for him to pull his head down for another kiss, he whispered, "Not yet."

And as she watched, he lowered his head to her breasts. His tongue drew lazy circles around the rigid tips of her nipples. One at a time, he lavished attention on the dark rosy buds. She shivered at the sensation and bit her lip to keep from moaning aloud.

But when he took first one nipple, then the other into his mouth, she lost that battle and whimpered helplessly. Again and again, he nibbled at her flesh with tender, gentle strokes of his teeth and tongue. Kathy arched high off the couch and made a grab for his shoulders, hoping to find something stable in her suddenly whirling universe.

He suckled her then, and Kathy felt his attentions right down to her toes. Over and over again, his lips and tongue tugged at her flesh, warming her and heating her blood beyond the boiling point. Deep within her, a pulsing ache began to build and she rocked her hips in time with it.

He seemed to sense what she needed because as his

mouth blissfully tortured her, he moved his right hand down, along her rib cage, across her abdomen to the fragile strip of elastic at the top of her panties. She ached, needing him to touch her, to ease the throbbing that had settled so firmly at her center.

As if knowing her every thought, he let his hand drop to cup her warmth. She groaned and tried to push her body into his touch. It was so much…and yet not nearly enough. She wanted him to touch her intimately. She wanted his fingers to slide over her damp heat and then dip within her. She wanted to feel him inside her body. And she wanted it now.

"Brian," she whispered, lifting her hips helplessly as his thumb scraped across the silky fabric of her panties to tease an especially sensitive spot of skin, "I need…"

He gave one of her nipples one last, sweeping kiss and swirl of his tongue before lifting his head to meet her gaze. "I know just what you need, Kath. I need it, too."

"Oh, thank heaven," she said on a choked off laugh. "I thought I might be alone in this."

"Not a chance, baby," he said with that crooked smile that had first caught her attention more than six weeks ago. "We're in this together. And we're about to be much more together than we are right now."

She stared into his eyes as he deftly smoothed her panties down and off. Kathy licked suddenly dry lips and waited, almost trembling, for what would come next.

She didn't have long to wait.

Brian stood up, stripped off his clothes and in what seemed like seconds, was back with her again. Warm, she thought as he covered her with his muscled body. So warm, so strong. She felt every lovely inch of him, his work-toughened body pressed to her own much-softer one. She looked up into his eyes as he moved to kneel between her legs.

Suddenly he stilled, a tight, hard expression on his face.

"What is it?" she asked, hoping to high heaven he wasn't having second thoughts. If he left her in this agitated state, she would have to kill him.

He stroked her updrawn legs, smoothing his palms against her skin, and she felt every callus, every work-worn scar, and shivered at the sensation.

"We can't."

It took a minute for his words to sink in, and when they did she swallowed hard and demanded. "Why not?"

That crooked smile of his appeared again as he said, "Because believe it or not, honey, I don't walk around every day carrying condoms on the off chance I might get lucky."

Condoms.

Stupid, that's what she was. She hadn't even considered protection.

"Don't suppose you have any?" he asked hopefully.

She shook her head. "Hasn't been a whole lot of call for them."

Brian nodded abruptly. "Though a part of me is

real glad to hear that, another part is what you might call…disappointed.''

Kathy's whole body felt as taut as a bow string, and yet she had the desperate urge to giggle. Who else would this happen to, if not her? Then she thought of something. "If you're only worried about pregnancy…"

"*Only?*" he echoed sardonically. "I'd like to remind you here that in the next room there's a living reminder of what can happen when you *don't* worry about pregnancy."

"I'm on the pill," she offered, and scooted closer to him. His hands continued to move on her legs, keeping that fire within blazing nicely. "To regulate my periods," she added, as if that was any of his business.

"Hmm…" He was thinking, and she could see the same spark of hope she felt, mirrored on his features. "Are you willing to take my word for it that I'm healthy?"

Right now she was willing to take his word for it that night was day. But she asked, "You said you never break your word, right?"

"Right."

"You give me your word everything's okay?"

"I do," he said solemnly, meeting her gaze with an intensity that torched her soul.

"Then I believe you, and for the record," she added, "I'm healthy, too."

"Thank heaven for the honor system," he said with feeling.

"Amen," she whispered.

Then, picking up where they had left off, he lowered one hand to her center and stroked the tender sensitive flesh between her thighs until Kathy thought she would lose what was left of her mind. She swiveled her hips against his hand and bumped into the back of the couch.

He chuckled hoarsely. "Wish we had more room," he said with a shake of his head.

"We could move to the floor," she offered, and hardly recognized her own voice.

"Next time," he promised. "Right now, all I can think about is being inside you. Feeling you surround me. I've wanted you from the moment we met, Kathy."

She knew that. Had known it all along. And now she could admit to something she wouldn't have owned up to six weeks ago.

"I wanted you, too," she said, staring up into those crystal-clear blue eyes. "From the minute you smiled at me the first time. I wanted this to happen."

A muscle in his jaw shook as he gritted his teeth hard. "Wish you'd have said something sooner, baby."

He dipped one finger into her depths.

"Oh, me, too," she said, and opened herself to him.

Over and over again, his fingers manipulated her, pushing her higher and higher until the air was so thin, she couldn't draw an easy breath. She knew he was watching her expressions as he tantalized her, and she didn't care. Kathy wanted him to know what he was doing to her. She wanted him to feel what she felt, to need what she needed.

And when she thought she couldn't get any higher, any closer to the edge that lay just beyond her reach, he withdrew his hand and joined his body to hers.

Brian entered her slowly, despite the rushing and roaring of his blood. Hunger fanned the flames of desire, and he was all but trembling with his need for her. And yet, he didn't want to miss a moment of this joining. He wanted to savor it, relish it for the gift it was.

Parting her thighs farther, he inched his way into her warmth. His head fell back on his neck and he let himself enjoy the slow, soft heat of her welcoming him. She lifted her hips and moaned. He knew what she was feeling. He felt it, too. And it was a first for him.

Never before had sex been like this. She touched him in places he hadn't known existed. Opening his eyes, he watched her liquid-chocolate eyes darken as he claimed her in the most elemental way. So tight, he thought. Tight and warm and so good. It felt as though he'd finally come home. And his home was within this one woman.

She winced as he joined their bodies fully, and though it cost him dearly, he paused long enough to ask, "Are you all right?"

Kathy nodded frantically, and cautiously rocked her hips against him. "Fine. Just...don't...stop..."

"Not for anything, baby," he said, and lowered

himself over her, supporting his weight with one hand firmly set on the arm of the couch above her head.

Then the magic took him and he gave himself up to it. Her breath dusted his cheek. Her nails scraped along his back. Her heels dug into the backs of his thighs as she arched into him over and over again. And he gave her all she wanted, needed, and then gave her more.

Again and again he retreated and advanced. His body moving to a new rhythm, he felt the familiar climb of anticipation. But this time there was more to it than simple release. This time he wanted her to know joy and wanted to see it register on her face. This time he wanted to give more than he took.

And when her first climax hit her, he felt the shuddering impact rock her body. He gritted his teeth against the wave of completion rising in him and held on to what was left of his control. He wanted to make this last, to draw out the magic, to take her to heights no man had ever taken her before.

When she sagged against the couch, depleted, a soft smile on her face, he leaned back, and she opened her eyes to look up at him.

"That was—" she paused for breath "—amazing."

"There's more," he promised.

"There couldn't be."

Then he touched her already-sensitized flesh and won a shiver from her that started at the top of her head and ended at her toes.

"Brian…"

"More," he said, calling up every ounce of self-control he'd ever possessed. His body ached, throbbed to join her in satisfaction, but he wouldn't allow it yet.

His thumb stroked the small nub of flesh at her center, and he smiled inwardly when she jolted in his arms and half came up off the couch to grab for him.

"Oh, my...oh, my..."

"Take it, Kathy," he whispered as he rubbed and stroked and caressed her into a fever pitch. Her hips rocked, her head twisted from side to side, and tremors snaked through her one after the other. "One more time, baby," he urged quietly. "Ride the wave one more time."

"It's too much," she managed to gasp as her eyes slid closed.

"It's never too much," he assured her. Her already-ravaged body was still poised near the brink. It didn't take long before pleasure claimed her for the second time.

She clutched at the sofa cushions, her hands fisting helplessly in the fabric. Her head tipped back; her mouth opened on a quiet moan as her body shook with the force of renewed delight.

"Brian..." she half cried out as she began her fall into oblivion.

"I'm right here, baby," he said, and pushed himself home, into her warmth, her welcome. And in a few, hard, quick strokes he reached the heights with her in time to float back to earth secure in the circle of her arms.

What could have been hours, but in reality was just a few minutes passed in stunned silence. Kathy loved the solid, warm feel of his body atop hers. She gloried in the heavy weight of him and enjoyed the press of his flesh against hers.

And she was darned impressed with her first taste of sexual intimacy.

Before she could stop herself, she murmured, "I never thought it would be like that."

"Hmm?"

"I mean," she continued, really talking more to herself than him, "I've read all the books, seen movies, listened to my friends talk, so I knew the basics going in..." She paused and chuckled weakly. "But the reality was so much more than anything I ever expected."

Brian levered himself up on one elbow and looked down at her. Why didn't he look as pleasantly relaxed as she felt?

"What do you mean, you've read all the books?"

She grinned and rubbed his shoulder. Amazing. So much muscle in one body. "You know," she said. "Books. Everything from self-help sexual manuals to romance novels. And," she pointed out, "I must say, romance novels are much closer to the truth about these things than anything else I've ever read."

Brian cleared his throat, shifted slightly and disengaged their bodies. Kathy groaned at his absence.

"Are you trying to tell me you're a virgin?" he asked incredulously.

"You mean you couldn't tell?" She stared up at

him and smiled even wider. "I think that's the nicest thing anyone's ever said to me."

"You are," he said in disbelief. "You are a virgin."

"Not anymore, thanks very much."

"Why didn't you say so?"

"It didn't seem relevant."

"Didn't seem—" He shook his head and scooted back from her to sit at the opposite end of the couch. Staring at her, he asked, "How could it not be relevant?"

Suddenly sensing that their closeness was at an end, Kathy scooted back into her corner of the couch and reached to the floor for the discarded afghan. Covering herself with it, she said, "I didn't ask you how many women you've slept with, did I?"

"No, but that's different."

"How?"

"It just is," he said tightly, and leaned over to grab up his clothes.

"So, if you'd known I was a virgin, this wouldn't have happened?"

He shot her a sardonic glance. "Oh, baby, it would have happened. But it would have happened differently."

"Then I'm glad you didn't know," she said shortly. "Because I wouldn't change a thing."

"Unbelievable," he muttered, and tugged on his shorts, then his uniform pants. "Your first time, you get tumbled on a too-short couch, and you think it's great."

"Would you rather I got tumbled on a couch and think it stunk?" she asked and really resented how he was robbing her of that pleasant glow she'd had only a moment ago.

"I'd *rather* have known so I could have been—"

"Better?" she finished for him.

Brian shot her another look, and this one seared her flesh right through the afghan like a laser beam. "Baby, it doesn't come much better than that."

A ripple of pleasure washed over her. "Then what's the problem?"

He stood up, and she watched the play of muscles on his bare back as he walked to the front window. Outside, dawn was beginning to streak the sky with soft shades of pink and lavender.

"I would have taken more care," he said softly, his back to her. "Been more gentle. Been more…I don't know. More *something*."

Her heart swelled. It was the only explanation she could think of to describe what she was feeling at the moment. He cared. Cared that she be happy and taken care of. And in a blinding flash Kathy realized just how much she cared for him. When had it happened? she wondered. When had she begun fostering all of these soft, fuzzy feelings for Sergeant Smile? She hadn't wanted to care about him. She'd wanted to keep him at arm's length. At a safe distance from her heart.

But somehow he'd sneaked past her defenses and now, she didn't even want to acknowledge how important he'd become to her. To her life.

She pushed off the couch, keeping the afghan securely wrapped around her. Walking across the room, she stopped beside him and laid one hand on his arm.

He turned and looked down at her.

"I'm a big girl, Brian," she said quietly.

One corner of his mouth lifted. "Believe me, I noticed."

Her lips twitched and she let herself enjoy the compliment hidden in those simple words. "I knew what I was doing and who I was doing it with."

"Yeah, but," he started to say.

"No buts," she interrupted. Soon she'd have to start figuring out what to do about the fact that she— good heavens—*loved* Brian Haley. But right now it was enough to stand here with him in the early-morning light and feel his arms come around her when she stepped up close.

"Kathy…" He planted a kiss on the top of her head, then rested his chin there. She tried to brace herself for whatever he was about to say even while wishing he wouldn't talk at all.

Fate took a hand then, in the form of Maegan's brief, disgruntled cry that clearly said, "I'm awake and hungry. Why is no one paying attention?"

Kathy smiled at the interruption and took the opportunity to turn and reach for the robe that had been tossed to the floor only a few, glorious minutes ago. As she dropped the afghan and slipped into the robe, tying the silk belt around her waist, she walked toward her bedroom. Brian was just a step or two behind her.

She opened the door and was met by Maegan's

teary-eyed, but smiling face. The little girl was standing up in the portable-crib, her tiny fists clutching at the railing. Her soft brown hair stood up in tangled tufts, and her one-piece sleeper was unzipped down to her round belly.

''Hi!'' the baby said proudly. She did enjoy using her extremely limited vocabulary.

''Hi, yourself,'' Kathy said as she walked toward the baby who was already reaching both arms up in a silent demand to be lifted out of bed.

Holding the tiny girl close, Kathy breathed in the milky, powdery scent that she would always associate with Maegan. Her heart turned over as the baby grinned up at her.

Brian stepped up behind her, and Maegan gave her daddy a toothsome smile, as well, clearly enjoying their undivided attention.

With the baby's warm, snuggly weight pressed against her heart and Brian's strong, stalwart presence right behind her, Kathy felt utterly and completely happy. And she realized that, despite all of her plans, she was in love with both the man and his daughter.

Brian reached past her to stroke his index finger down Maegan's cheek, and as he did he whispered, ''We have to talk, Kathy.''

''We will,'' she said, tightening her grip on the baby. They would have to talk. About a lot of things. But, she decided, their talk wouldn't come until she'd found time to do some serious thinking.

Nine

"**I** may be in big trouble," Kathy confessed, reaching for her margarita glass.

"Now there's a nice start to the evening's conversation," Tina said, and crossed her arms on the table. Leaning forward, she demanded, "Explain."

Explain? Kathy thought. How in the heck could she explain something she had only just figured out herself? She took a long, deep gulp of the slushy drink and felt the icy coldness sweep through her. And still it did little to quench the warmth that had been with her all day.

Warmth? Nope, wrong word. *Unbelievably hot, blazing flames* would be a better description. All she'd had to do all day was remember how she'd started out

her morning, and an explosion of heat that made
Mount Saint Helens look like a peashooter completely
swamped her.

She felt the flush rising in her cheeks and deliberately turned away from Tina's too-knowing gaze. Taking a moment to get her hormones back under control,
Kathy slowly looked around Tio Taco, her favorite
Mexican restaurant. Brilliant splashes of yellow, or-
ange and green decorated the large room. Bouquets of
fresh flowers adorned every table, and overhead, piña-
tas and decorative gourds hung from rough-hewn
beams. In the far corner a lone guitarist provided
lovely melodies that floated over the crowd, urging
quiet conversation and relaxation.

Relaxation. She almost laughed out loud. Heck, she
hadn't been relaxed since Brian Haley had moved in
across the hall.

"You're stalling," Tina said.

Caught, Kathy thought, and turned her head to look
at her friend. "I know."

"So, spill."

"I don't know where to start."

Tina picked up her own drink and sat back. Waving
her margarita glass in a toast salute, she said before
taking a long drink, "Start smack in the middle of the
most interesting part."

"We made love on my couch this morning."

Tina choked and covered her mouth with one hand
to keep from spitting margarita across the table.
Coughing and gagging, she fought for breath.

Kathy half stood up, moving to slap her friend on

the back, when Tina waved her into her seat and shook her head.

"I'm...okay..." she said between quick gasps of air. "But geez, you should warn a person before throwing these things out there."

"Sorry." Embarrassed beyond belief, Kathy took another gulp of her drink and muttered, "I can't imagine why I even told you that."

"I'd be offended if you hadn't," Tina quipped, and leaned forward again eagerly. "This is big news and I want to hear everything about it. But first things first," she said. "Who was the lucky man? The marine?"

"Nobody but."

Tina smiled and practically purred. "Details, Kath, details."

"It was..." She paused, searching for the right word.

"Great? Magnificent?" Tina tried to help. "Earth shaking?"

About a dozen more adjectives, each more glowing than the other ought to about cover it. Heck, just talking about the experience had her insides in a twist and her mouth going dry. "All of the above."

"Wow." Tina propped her chin in her hand and sighed.

"Why are you acting as if you've never done it?" Kathy asked, a bit uncomfortable with Tina's obvious enthusiasm for her sex life. "I've seen your children. I know you have."

Tina waved her hand again and grinned. "I love Ted, but that's married sex. This is *interesting* sex."

Oh, for heaven's sake.

Kathy dismissed Tina's unexpected bawdy streak for the moment; the woman was missing the real point here.

"This isn't about the sex," Kathy said quietly.

If anything, Tina looked more interested than ever, her twin blond eyebrows forming high arches. "There's more?"

"I think I'm—" She stopped, shook her head and started again. No point in saying this at all if she wasn't going to be honest. No matter how terrifying the reality of the situation was. "Nope, I lied. I *know* I'm falling in love with him."

"All *right!*" Tina crowed and pumped one fist in the air as if she was at a high school football game cheering for a touchdown.

A few people glanced their way and Kathy gave them all a tight smile before glaring at her best friend. "I appreciate the enthusiasm," she said, "but put the pom-poms away, okay?"

"Oops, sorry," the other woman said, but she didn't look sorry. "But this really is a red-letter day. You're finally in love! When do Ted and I get to meet him?"

Another problem. Did she really want to start inviting Brian into the rest of her life? Was she ready for her friends to meet him? For people to see them as a couple? Why would she do that, when she wasn't even sure yet what lay between them? No, it was better to keep this thing, whatever it was, as quiet as possible, until she knew one way or the other what was going to happen.

Besides, she wasn't about to admit to Brian that she loved him. That would open up a can of worms that Kathy simply wasn't ready to face yet. And with her best friend's capacity for "loose lips," getting her and Brian together sounded like a bad idea all the way around.

"I know that look," Tina said, frowning. "You're going to keep him all to yourself, aren't you?"

"It's not that simple."

"Sure it is. Either you love him, or you're just using him for sex."

The truth was it was both of those things.

"This is serious, Tina."

"You bet it is and it's high time, if you ask me."

"I knew you'd say that."

"Well, think about it, Kath." Tina picked up her drink, took a swallow and reached for the bowl of tortilla chips in the middle of the table. Stabbing the air with one of the chips, she said, "Not only have you left the ranks of the vestal virgins, but you've done it with the man you love. What could be better?"

Just about anything, she thought but didn't say. Sex was one thing. Love, for pity's sake, was quite another. Good heavens, you'd think Tina would understand what she was going through better than anyone.

"You know how I feel about this," she said. "I didn't want to love anyone."

"Because of your mom."

She said it as though it meant nothing.

"Are you going to sit there and try to tell me that's not reason enough to steer clear of any entanglements?"

"Yes."

Kathy set her drink down, leaned back against the butter-yellow leather booth seat and folded her arms across her chest. "How can you say that? My mother is a serial bride."

Tina actually chuckled at that. "That doesn't mean you will be, too."

"Darn right," she snapped. "I'm not going to get married just so I can get divorced and screw up my kids' lives."

Tina eyed her sternly. "So you think I will? Not all marriages end in divorce, y'know."

"No, only half."

"So, be in the 'till death do us part' half."

"What a keen idea," Kathy quipped. "But don't you think everyone who gets married figures themselves to be in that half?"

"Sure, but it isn't the luck of the draw that lands you in the 'keeper' half, you know."

"I know," she said.

"I don't think you do," Tina said and leaned forward again, staring Kathy in the eyes and silently daring her to look away. "Marriage isn't easy. Nothing worthwhile is. You have to work at it. You have to want to make it last. You have to give it everything you've got. A lot of divorces happen because two people got tired of trying."

Visions of her mother, Spring, rose up in Kathy's mind. True, Spring didn't usually stick around once the bloom was off the rose, so to speak.

"I realize that, but there are others. You and Ted, for example. You guys don't have to work at it."

"Ha!" Tina smiled broadly and shook her head. "You think Ted came to me the way he is now? Hardly. I trained him. Just like he trained me. Most of the rough spots are gone now, but they still crop up from time to time."

Kathy couldn't even imagine Ted and Tina having rough spots. Their marriage was based on friendship. They actually *liked* each other as much as they loved. "Another bubble burst," she murmured.

"You want life in a bubble or reality?"

"The bubble," Kathy muttered.

"You think too much," Tina said with a soft smile. "What you should be doing is *feeling*. If you love him, don't run away."

Her fingers swirled through the water ring on the heavily varnished tabletop. "But there's no guarantee it would work."

Tina munched her chip and grabbed another. "Honey, there's no guarantees about *anything*. Heck, a meteor could crash through the roof of this restaurant in five minutes and take out all of us."

Kathy smiled reluctantly. "And the chances of that are…?"

Her friend shrugged. "Doesn't really matter, does it?" Tina asked. "It could happen."

Possible, but not probable. While marriage, on the

other hand, was a real risk no matter how you looked at it.

"You're missing another point in this," she said.

"Which is?"

"Our whole relationship is based on his need for help with Maegan."

"You love her, don't you?"

"Oh, yeah." Being with Maegan satisfied every maternal urge she'd ever had. The baby had become a huge part of her life. And the thought of not seeing her grow up…not being around to see her first day of school, her first date, her first dance, broke her heart. If she walked away from Brian, she'd be walking away from that baby, too. Still… "But that's no basis for a relationship."

"There have been worse ones. Besides, maybe it started out that way, but—"

"But what?" Kathy asked, shaking her head again for emphasis. "Nothing's really changed. I still watch Maegan. He goes to work, comes home, picks up the baby…"

"Makes love with you on the couch…" Tina added.

"Once," Kathy said, then corrected, "okay, twice."

"Twice?" Tina sighed again. "Oh, you gotta love this guy."

"That's the problem, though, isn't it?"

"Not really. Your choices are ridiculously easy." Tina held up two fingers and ticked them off as she went on. "One, you snatch up the marine and enjoy what you've found."

"Or...?"

"Or you turn your back on love and any chance at happily ever after because of what *might* happen."

"I'd like to remind you at this point that I'll be going to Vegas in little more than a week to witness my mother's *sixth* wedding."

Tina smiled. "Amazing that a woman so devoted to finding love could raise a woman so determined to avoid it."

Their waitress arrived with their order, and after setting down two steaming platters of enchiladas, rice and beans, left them again.

"I just don't know what to do," Kathy whispered.

Tina leaned across the table and patted her hand. "Do me a favor. For once in your life, Kath...follow your heart, not your head."

As her friend started eating, Kathy thought about what she'd said. She was tempted, so tempted. But she knew her heart would lead her to the one place she'd always been afraid of going. Love and marriage.

And she wasn't at all sure she was strong enough to take the risk.

Brian stepped into the empty hallway again, scanning the brightly lit corridor for signs that Kathy had come home. But everything was quiet. Too damned quiet, he thought for the thousandth time that night.

Maegan, perched on his hip, seemed to pick up on

his mood and sniffled. A sure sign that a rip-roaring cryfest was on its way.

Automatically he jiggled her slightly, acknowledging that over the past two weeks, he'd gotten pretty good at this whole baby thing. Not to mention the fact that he'd fallen completely in love with his daughter. He smiled as he looked at her pouty face. Was it just him? Or was she really as gorgeous as he thought?

As if in answer, Maegan's mouth scrunched up and a pitiful cry worked its way loose.

"It's okay, sweetie," he whispered. "Nothing to worry about. Kathy'll be home soon."

She rubbed both hands across her eyes and laid her head down on his shoulder.

"Tired, aren't you?" he asked, and walked back into his apartment and closed the door. "Well, I think I can take care of *your* problem, anyway."

Together they went to the kitchen where Brian pulled a bottle of milk out of the fridge. Briefly he stared at the shelves that used to hold only a couple of bottles of beer and the fixings for sandwiches. Now there was a half dozen jars of baby food, enough milk to start his own dairy and lots of healthy things, like vegetables. And fruit.

"A lot of changes in two short weeks," he muttered, realizing that that statement covered a whole lot more territory than just his refrigerator. He was a father now. And a man deeply in lust. But even as the word *lust* entered his mind, he altered it. He wasn't really sure what he was feeling, but he knew damn well it was more than just simple hormone hockey.

Oh, he wanted Kathy, no doubt about it. But he also enjoyed listening to her talk. He liked watching her hold the baby. It gave him a good feeling to come home at the end of a long, hard day dealing with knot-headed recruits and see her smile.

"She got past my perimeter," he muttered thickly. "Outflanked me, outmaneuvered me and won the field." He'd wanted an affair, like every other relationship he'd ever had. But what he'd gotten was more. So much more that he wasn't sure he was really ready to define it. Even to himself.

Maegan slapped his jaw with one little fist, as if reminding him to get the darn milk warmed up.

"Right," he said, nodding. "Baby's problems first, then Daddy's." He stuck the bottle inside the small appliance and said, "God bless microwaves."

As the milk heated, he sat Maegan on the counter and kept one hand on her belly to keep her in place. Her little heels battered against the cabinets below, letting him know her patience was nearly at an end.

"It's not just your bottle you're wanting, is it?" he asked. "You miss Kathy, too, don't you?" Brian smoothed one hand across her downy hair and along her back in a soft caress.

The baby hiccuped.

"She's become your mommy, hasn't she?" He should have known that Kathy would become as important to the baby as she had to him. Of course Maegan missed her. Kathy was the true constant in her life. He came and went, usually seeing her only first thing in the morning and last thing at night. Except for the weekends, which they'd been spending with Kathy, anyway.

"We're in deep, aren't we, Mae?" he asked in a quiet, husky voice.

The baby responded with another sniffle, just as the microwave beeper announced it had finished working. He grabbed the bottle and lifting Maegan, headed for the living room. Sitting down on the couch, he held his little girl while she drank her evening snack and let his mind wander to Kathy again. Lately, its favorite pastime.

"She's actually on a date," he said, and heard the tightness in his voice. "She's out spending time with that other guy despite what happened between us this morning."

Maegan ignored him, concentrating instead on holding her bottle and sucking down the milk as fast as she could.

"I thought we made a...connection, Maegan. I thought what we shared hit her as hard as it hit me." He shook his head and stared at the wall opposite him. "How in the hell—excuse me, heck—could she go on a date after that?"

Maegan abruptly threw her bottle and let out a fitful cry.

"Way to go, Sarge," he muttered, standing up to walk his daughter. "Upset the kid because you can't get Kathy out of your mind."

It didn't improve his mood any to realize he was feeling like a jealous boyfriend. Jealous. Him? Damn right, he thought. He wanted a look at the guy Kathy was dating. Actually, to be accurate, he wanted one clean punch at the guy.

A knock on the door splintered that pleasant image.

Carrying Maegan, he walked across the room, opened the door and stared blankly at the woman he'd just been thinking about.

Kathy'd heard Maegan crying as she walked down the hall to her apartment. And in seconds she'd found herself standing in front of the door instead of her own. She told herself that she was only doing this for Maegan's sake. That she wanted to help ease the baby. But even *she* wasn't believing that. She knew darn well that the reality of the situation was she wanted…no, *needed* to see Brian.

Everything Tina had said to her was still rocketing around inside her brain. She had to find out if Brian had been as affected by their lovemaking as she had. She had to know if he felt for her what she was feeling for him.

But now that she was here, all she could do was look at him. Barefoot, he wore faded blue jeans that hugged his long legs. A red T-shirt, stamped USMC, strained across his broad chest, and a faint shadow of whisker stubble stained his cheeks. His blue eyes seemed to simmer with all kinds of dangerously wicked thoughts, and her stomach pitched just imagining them.

"Hi," she said, wishing she could think of something more, yet immensely grateful that her voice had worked at all.

"Hi, back," Brian said, a slight frown on his face. "You're home early."

"Yeah." She stepped into the apartment as he moved aside, silently inviting her in. Just brushing against him as she walked was enough to make her palms damp and her insides quiver. He closed the door behind her as she took Maegan from him. Dropping her purse on the nearest chair, Kathy soothed the baby with whispered words and gentle strokes up and down her back.

In seconds the little girl was quiet again. It was as if all she'd needed was to hear the sound of Kathy's voice. That knowledge wrapped itself around her heart and warmed her right down to her soul. This tiny child had made Kathy a part of her life. An important part.

Brian retrieved the bottle from the carpet and handed it over as Kathy took the baby to her crib. He'd noticed how easily Maegan had settled down as soon as the woman she obviously considered her mother had shown up. The two females shared some sort of bond that he apparently wasn't a part of. A twinge of regret settled in the pit of his stomach as he admitted that it bothered him to realize how much that bothered him.

When Kathy came out of the bedroom and pulled the door closed before looking at him, he asked, "Is she sleeping?"

"Out like a light."

"Good," he said, letting his gaze drift up and down the length of her. She wore a deep-green blouse with a low, scooped neck, a black skirt and black nylons that he wanted to strip off her with his teeth. Hardly a sexpot kind of outfit, he told himself, then wondered why he was suddenly so hungry for her that he felt as though his body would burst right through the fabric of his jeans.

No, he told himself. What they needed to do was talk. He wanted to know who in the hell she was dating. And he wanted to know *why* she was dating one guy and making love with *him*. He wanted to tell her how nuts it made him to think of her kissing, holding someone else.

"I, uh," she said, under his steady regard, "maybe I should go."

A quick burst of panic lit up his insides like mortar fire on a still, cold night. The thought of her leaving him at that moment made him want to grab her and never let her go.

The hell with talking.

"No, don't," he said quickly, desperately. "Don't leave."

"Brian…" She shook her head helplessly, and he read the hunger in her eyes easily, since he was feeling the same damned thing.

He crossed to her in a few long strides. Grabbing her, he pulled her close and wrapped both arms around her, holding her tightly enough to imprint the form of her body on his own. And still, it wasn't close enough. He wanted to be a part of her again. To feel himself held deeply within her. To watch her eyes glaze over with passion and to know that *he* could give her that. That they shared what seemed like pure magic to him.

All day, memories had taunted him, tortured him. He'd barely gotten his work done and still didn't remember the drive home. All he could think of was Kathy. All he wanted was her. And more of that magic.

Her hands splayed against his back, he felt her warmth enter him and ease the dark loneliness he'd been feeling all evening. It felt so right to be here with her. It *was* right, he thought. In so many ways.

"I've missed you," he murmured and kissed the top of her head.

"Me, too," she said, her voice muffled against his chest.

"I need you," he said.

"Me, too," Kathy whispered, tilting her head back to look up at him.

He bent lower, brushed his lips across hers, then tugged at her bottom lip with the edges of his teeth. "I want you," he said hoarsely. "Now."

"Oh, me, too," Kathy said with a nod. Then as he eased them both over to his couch, she added, "This is crazy, you know."

"Crazy," he agreed. "And wonderful."

"Oh, yeah," she said as he pulled her down onto the cushions. "That, too."

Ten

Kathy kept her arms looped around his neck as he lowered her to the couch. One corner of her mind chuckled at the fact that they'd yet to find themselves in an actual *bed* together. Although, Brian's couch was substantially wider and longer than her own, and briefly she wondered if he'd coaxed many other women down onto its lush cushions. But a moment later all thoughts but one died as his hands skimmed up her legs, inching her skirt hem higher up her thighs before retreating along her calves and down to her ankles.

She gazed up at him, backlit by the soft, dim light of a lamp on the table at the far end of the sofa. Moonlight, too, poured in through the slatted blinds and lay in a pattern of straight lines across the floor. From somewhere in the apartment she heard a clock ticking, and the slow, steady beat kept time with the pounding of her heart.

The gentle scrape of Brian's palms against her nylon-clad legs felt sinfully good and effectively shut down her mind. She sighed heavily and let her eyes slide shut so that she could concentrate more completely on just what he was doing to her.

She felt him slip her shoes off and stroke her arches with the pads of his thumbs. Goose bumps raced along her flesh, and she shivered, rubbing her back against the overstuffed cushions beneath her.

"Man," he whispered, his fingers once again sliding up the length of her legs. "I love these black nylons."

First thing tomorrow, she told herself, she would order a case of the darned things.

He placed a kiss on the inside of her knee, and Kathy sucked in a gulp of air through gritted teeth. Watery. Her entire body felt like liquid, pooling beneath his hands. He worked his mouth along the inside of her thigh, moving higher, higher. She lifted her hips slightly and let her legs fall apart, inviting him closer.

His hands slid up her legs and stopped when he encountered smooth flesh at the tops of her stockings. "Help me, I'm a dying man," he murmured. "Not panty hose, stockings."

She opened her eyes and looked down to find him admiring the lacy edge of her black hose. "Stockings are better than panty hose?'' she asked, and felt a dazed smile curve her mouth.

Brian slipped one finger beneath the top of one thigh-high nylon and smoothed it across her flesh, sending a ripple of anticipation ebbing through her bloodstream. "Oh, yeah," he told her, that lazy, crooked grin on his face. "Stockings are *much* better. The kind with garters, best of all."

"I'll remember that," she said, and adjusted her mental shopping list accordingly. Instantly an image rose up in her mind. Her, wearing a black garter belt, stockings and little else, while Brian Haley stood behind her, admiring every inch of her with his amazing hands.

Dizzy with the imagery, she hardly noticed when Brian worked the buttons of her blouse free and undid the zipper on her skirt. He slipped her clothes from her body effortlessly, leaving her lying on the couch wearing nothing but her stockings and panties.

Then the dream image faded as she watched him hungrily. Her body felt poised like a long distance runner ready to start the most important race of her career. Brian reached up and stroked her center through the filmy, sheer fabric of her black panties.

Kathy's body jerked in reaction, then rejoiced again as he repeated the caress. Sensation, hot and fluid, whirled inside her, and she fought to keep her eyes open and fixed on him. She didn't want to miss a moment of this night. She wanted it imprinted on her memory for all time. His thumb moved over her most-sensitive piece of flesh, and she bit back a soft moan that was half distress and half pleading.

Now she knew what it was that awaited her at the end of passion's long road. Now she looked forward eagerly to that mind-numbing explosion of sensation. She wanted to feel him inside her again. She wanted to explore his mouth with her own. She wanted to taste his breath and relearn the secrets of his body. And she wanted it all, now. It felt like years since she'd last held him inside her depths. Reaching for him, she clutched at his shoulders and tried to pull him toward her for a kiss.

But he shook his head and loosened her hold on him. Disappointment shuddered through her as her hands opened and closed on the cushions beneath her. What was he up to? Why didn't he want to kiss her and join their bodies as badly as she did?

"There's no rush tonight, Kathy," he whispered, stroking one finger across her abdomen, just above the top of her panties.

She swallowed hard. He wanted it, too. He just wanted to go slowly. She didn't know whether to be pleased or frustrated.

"Tonight," Brian went on, meeting her gaze, "I'm going to give you the experience you should have had your first time."

Kathy wished he would stop fretting over that. She'd enjoyed every minute of their time together the night before, and if she could only find her voice, she'd tell him so.

He hooked his fingers beneath the narrow band of

elastic at the top of her panties and as she watched him, still unaccountably mute, he slowly pulled them down and off her legs. He tossed the scrap of black lace aside then and reached for her. His hands closed over her naked hips and pulled her along the couch, closer to him, as he lifted her bottom off the cushions.

"Brian?" His name came out in a hoarse croak of sound, and Kathy cleared her throat hoping to do better.

"Relax, honey," he whispered, as he lifted her hips easily in his two big hands.

Relax? With his fingers kneading the soft flesh of her behind? With her thighs parted and her legs dangling helplessly a foot above the couch? Oh, she didn't think relaxing was a reasonable hope at the moment.

"Brian," she said, and this time heard her voice sound clear and strong. She might have been a virgin until the night before, but she wasn't stupid. She knew exactly what he was about to do and wasn't at all sure she was ready for that just yet. The embarrassment level alone was mind-boggling. She reached for him, but he only smiled as he bent his head to her center.

The instant his mouth touched her body, Kathy forgot everything she had been determined to say. Things like, "What are you doing?" or "Put me down." A delicious spiral of heat uncoiled in the pit of her stomach and slowly spread to every inch of her body. Like an incoming tide, she felt it rise and rise as Brian's mouth took her to places she'd never dreamed existed.

Much to her surprise, she found that she was more than ready for this latest lesson in making love.

Keeping her gaze fixed on him, she forced herself to watch as he pleasured her. He slid his tongue along her almost-too-sensitive flesh again and again and each time, Kathy thought she would lose her mind to the overwhelming sensations rocketing around inside her.

His hands, his mouth, his hot breath against her flesh, all these things combined to throw what was left of Kathy's nice, safe world into turmoil. Everything she'd said to Tina only hours before flashed across her mind, and she called herself a fool. She didn't *think* she was in love with this man. She *knew* it. Deep in her heart, she'd always known it. From the moment she'd seen him, a part of her must have recognized that this was the man who could breach her defenses. This was the man she wouldn't be able to hide from.

She couldn't even remember what her life had been like before Brian Haley. Didn't want to remember the lonely nights, the empty dreams. She wanted this night, this moment to go on forever.

But moments pass one into the other, and soon she felt the cataclysmic end racing toward her. Her breath came in short, harsh gasps. Every square inch of her body felt gloriously alive. Something inside her tightened, like an overwound spring. Her hands fisted on the couch cushions, hanging on as tightly as though she were dangling on the edge of a precipice.

And with one more slow, languid stroke of his

tongue, Brian sent her flying over that edge, with sky-rockets bursting behind her closed eyelids.

Brian watched as the passion claimed her. He filled his heart and mind with the soft sounds of her cries, with the reflexive jerk of her body in his hands. And as the last tremor slowly eased through her, he set her down gently onto the couch. Quickly he tore off his clothes and lay down over her before sliding his body into hers.

Her eyes flew open and she gazed up at him, wonderstruck. An instant later she looped her arms around his neck and pulled him closer. He felt her stocking-clad legs come around his hips, and the cool, slick sensation sent shock waves pulsing through him. It had taken every ounce of his self-control to contain his own needs while servicing hers. And now that he was a part of her again, his own release was thrumming in his ears. This would be fast, he knew. Hard and fast and wickedly welcome.

He moved within her, advancing, retreating. His gaze locked with hers, and he looked deeply into the warm chocolate eyes that seemed to hold all the secrets of the world. How could he not have seen it before this? How could he have pretended, even to himself, that what they had was temporary? A fleeting thing? This was deep and real and so damned good it terrified the hell out of him.

For the first—and last—time in his life, Brian Haley was in love. The word ricocheted off the walls of his mind, letting him know that sooner or later he would have to deal with this discovery. But not now, he told himself, and that was the last coherent thought he had before his body erupted and he poured his heart, his soul, his everything, into her warmth.

What felt like an eternity later Brian reluctantly eased himself away from Kathy only long enough to roll onto his side and pull her closely to him. Then, lying together, her back to his front, they watched the moonlit shadows.

She shivered and he held her more closely. "Cold?" he asked in a whisper of sound.

Kathy sighed and shook her head, pillowed on his arm. "In a way, I don't think I'll ever be cold again."

"I know just how you feel," he said, his breath ruffling her hair.

"I don't know if you can," she said, half turning in his arms to look up at him.

Brian studied her features, noted the troubled gleam in her eyes and felt his heart catch at the sight. "We're not talking about being cold, are we?"

"Not entirely," she murmured.

"Is there a problem?" he asked, hoping there was a dragon somewhere he could slay for her. He ached to see worry on her face so soon after what could only be described as a miraculous joining.

She ran the flat of her hand across his chest and he felt her touch like a fiery brand. Amazing. Already his body was up and raring to go again. But he forced his desire back under control when she started talking.

"I never expected to find…" She paused as if looking for just the right word. Then she sighed, met his gaze and said simply, "You."

And she didn't look real happy about having found him, either, he thought, but he didn't say.

"What we have together," she continued, with a sad, confused expression coloring her features, "is special, but scary, too."

Scary? Hell, it was downright terrifying. And brother, it took some doing for a marine to admit to being scared.

"Believe me, honey," he said, "I do know what you're feeling."

"Maybe on some level," she agreed. "But, Brian..." She stopped, then started again. "Did you say your mom still lives in the neighborhood where you grew up?"

Okay, now *he* was the confused party here. "Yeah, but—"

"And your folks, they were happy?" she asked. "I mean, in their marriage?"

He nodded. "They had fights like everyone else, but yeah. They were happy. Still would be if my dad hadn't died a few years ago."

She nodded and idly stroked his chest again. If she knew what her touch did to him, she would stop if she expected conversation. Except there was something about her now that seemed so haunted, so sad, it made Brian forget about everything but the need to comfort her somehow.

"What is it?" he asked, and stroked one hand along her spine.

Instead of answering his question, she asked one of her own. "You probably figured on getting married one day, right?"

He'd never really given it much thought, until recently, and he knew that wasn't the right thing to say at the moment, so he said only, "I suppose so."

"Well, I never did," she said. Staring up into his eyes, Kathy told him about her mother, Spring. About how Kathy had grown up knowing that marriages didn't last. That men left and love disappeared.

His blue eyes stared deeply into hers as she tried to make him see how confused she was about this thing they'd found together. And when she'd finished telling her story, Kathy said, "I...*care* for you, Brian. More than anyone I've ever known."

He squeezed her briefly, and she took some small comfort in the strength of his embrace.

"But I don't know what to do about this situation."

Brian shifted one hand to cup her cheek, his thumb stroking along the line of her cheekbone. She turned her face into his palm, absorbing the warmth of him and claiming it.

"Believe it or not," he said, a small smile touching one corner of his mouth, "I don't know what to do, either. About you and me. About Maegan."

Kathy blinked and looked up at him. Maegan? She could understand feeling strange about *their* relationship, but not this. How could he be confused about his daughter? What was there to decide? He loved the baby. She knew he did. She'd seen him with the little girl who so clearly had claimed his heart. Maegan was a part of his life now. Surely, she thought, he couldn't turn his back on a helpless child?

"What do you mean you're confused about Maegan?" she asked, her own problems forgotten for the moment.

He must have noticed a fighting spark in her eyes because he smiled briefly. "Don't hit me, champ," he said. "This isn't about wanting to keep her with me. Of course I'm keeping her. I love her."

He said the words so simply, Kathy was convinced. But if he wasn't worried about that, then what?

Brian reached up and scraped one hand along the top of his head. Staring at the ceiling, he said softly, "You're not the only one whose life has had some major changes lately."

"True," she said, "but I still don't understand."

"Deployment."

Kathy knew that word as well as anyone else who lived in a military town would. Marines were sent all over the world for six months at a time or longer, leaving their families behind to fend for themselves. Deployment.

She hadn't even considered it before this, and now, the very idea of him being gone for six long months was enough to make her want to cling to him tightly.

Not to mention the fact that when he next left, Maegan would be alone.

He glanced at her and frowned. "What do I do about Maegan when I ship out?"

She didn't know what to say. Her first impulse of course, was to shout, "Leave her with me." But she didn't have the right. They weren't married. Heck, she wasn't sure what they were.

"I could leave her with my mother or one of my sisters," he continued, and a part of Kathy cringed away from the thought of not only losing Brian, but Maegan, for months on end.

"But if I did, I'd have to sign over guardianship to them," he continued, almost to himself. "The military won't leave a child behind who's unprotected legally. And there's the whole thing about handing her over to people who would only be strangers to her. Should I really upset her whole world again?"

The tension in his voice reached her, and she realized that as confused as she was, his problems were far greater. "Could you choose to *not* be deployed?"

He laughed shortly and shook his head. "Nope. Oh, there are battalions that don't usually deploy. But *every* marine, from the rawest recruit to the most desk-bound general must be *able* to deploy at a moment's notice. If you can't deploy, you can't be a marine."

"Surely they would make an exception in an emergency," she said.

Brian snorted and shook his head. "No exceptions. I know a first lieutenant whose wife died. He had no one to leave his kids with when he deployed, so he had to resign." He paused and added, "We all know the rules. No exceptions."

Kathy heard the grim tone of his voice and knew instinctively what leaving the corps would mean to him.

"Being a marine is who I am," Brian said, unknowingly reinforcing her thoughts. "It's all I've ever wanted to be. Don't know what I'd do as a civilian."

Her mind racing, Kathy tried to find an answer to the problem, but the only one she could come up with was for Brian to get married so Maegan would be taken care of. But the thought of marrying him herself was frightening, and the idea of someone *else* marrying him was unacceptable, so she didn't have a clue what to say.

Finally she asked, almost afraid of the answer, "When do you deploy again?"

"That's the one bright spot in all this," he told her with a sigh. "Not for another six months, so at least I have time to come up with something brilliant."

Not much time, though, she thought, knowing that the next six months would fly by. And as she tried to imagine her world without Brian and Maegan Haley in it, Kathy fell into a restless sleep. Not even the warm strength of Brian's arms wrapped around her kept the aching loneliness of her dreams at bay.

The next morning found Brian Haley, gunnery sergeant, kneeling in the sand beside a laughing little girl in pink overalls as she waited impatiently for him to make the park swing move.

"Now, darlin'," he said, his big, suddenly clumsy fingers trying to fix the shoulder strap of her ruffled bib overalls, "if you don't sit still, we'll never get this done."

It would have been easier on both of them, he thought, if Kathy had come with them. But she'd opted to stay at home and catch up on the work she hadn't been getting done. At least, that's what she'd said when he'd invited her along. But he had the feeling there was more to it than that. Brian frowned slightly as he remembered the look on her face when she woke up only a couple of hours ago.

They'd spent the night on his sofa wrapped in each other's arms, and if her haunted eyes were any indication, she'd gotten as little sleep as he had.

Tormented with the thought of deploying and leaving not only his daughter but Kathy behind, Brian had slept fitfully, plagued by dream images of himself, alone and miserable.

He wondered if Kathy had been feeling the same things.

Maegan kicked her little legs, landing a lucky blow to his knee. He rubbed the spot and laughed shortly, pushing his other problems aside. "Okay, okay, I get the message. Less thinking, more playing."

The baby giggled, and he silently wondered at the miracle of it all. This tiny person had been born into the world because he'd been careless. And now he couldn't help but think it hadn't been carelessness at all, but Fate, with a capital *F*. Brian couldn't imagine not having Maegan in his life. Any more than he could stomach the thought of being without Kathy.

At that he caught himself and returned his attentions to his daughter. For the moment he would concentrate on Maegan and leave the rest of the confusion aside for a bit. Maybe by not thinking about it, a solution would come to him.

And maybe Kathy just needed a little time for some thinking herself.

After strapping Maegan in, Brian stepped around behind his daughter and gave her well-padded bottom a small push. Instantly that rush of giggles exploded from her belly and rose up in the clear air to settle over him like a blessing.

Again and again he pushed her, barely sending the swing moving at all, but it was enough to please Maegan. Brian scanned the rest of the playground, noting the moms, dads and kids sprinkled across the sandy spot in the middle of Bayside Park. Happy squeals and the occasional cry sounded out as children fought over the log castle and the brightly painted ponies on stiff springs. A soft breeze dusted across the open spaces and carried the scent of the nearby ocean.

It was a great day that would have been perfect if Kathy had been with them. With her, the three of them would have seemed like just another happy family, like the others here at the park.

"Bri?"

A too familiar voice shattered the pleasant imagery in his mind and Brian turned slowly around to face the woman speaking to him.

"Bri!" She said again and added, "It *is* you!"

Dana, long, blond hair in a ponytail, makeup perfect and dressed in a sports bra and running shorts tiny enough to make any red-blooded man whimper for mercy, stood staring at him as if she'd seen a ghost.

He hadn't seen her since the night he'd left her place before dinner—or anything else—could happen.

"Hi," Brian said, and congratulated himself silently on his eloquence.

"You've been bad," Dana said with a slow shake of her head. "You never called to apologize for leaving me so abruptly."

He shrugged and mentally noted that her blue eyes looked just a little cold and hard around the edges. Had they always been like that? "I figured you weren't speaking to me."

"Well." She turned on the pout he would always associate with her, and he wondered why it didn't have the same appeal anymore. "I was upset, but I'll forgive you."

She took a step closer, and Brian's hand curled around the swing's chains, bringing Maegan's ride to a sudden halt.

In response the little girl let loose a disgruntled screech.

Dana shot the child an annoyed look before turning her gaze back to Brian. "What on earth are *you* doing at the park?"

He'd never thought of Dana as a rocket scientist or anything, but surely even she could see he was pushing a child in a swing. "Entertaining Maegan."

She looked at the baby again and took a small instinctive step backward. "Baby-sitting? *You?*"

The complete disbelief in her voice irritated him. All right, so he wouldn't have believed it himself a month ago, but people could change, couldn't they?

"I'm not baby-sitting," he said tightly.

"Then what...?"

He glanced down at the baby to see a scowl on her face that was so much like his own he chuckled before looking back at the woman he'd once dated. "This is my daughter, Maegan. Maegan, this is Dana."

The two females looked at each other with equal measures of dislike. But Dana broke free first to stare at Brian. "Your *daughter?*"

"Yeah."

"But you didn't tell me you had a…a…"

"Baby?" He finished the sentence for her. "I didn't know myself until a couple of weeks ago."

Dana all but shivered. Still backing up as if she thought parenthood might be contagious, she started running in place. "Look, it was, uh, nice to see you again," she said lamely, although her expression said it had been anything but. Then she glanced at her watch. "Wow. Look at the time. I've got to run. See you sometime," she said, and lifted one hand as she took off across the park at a dead sprint.

Brian stared after her for a long minute. Dana hadn't been able to get away fast enough. And the look on her face when she saw Maegan. How could she not have been drawn in by such a pretty baby? He shook his head and wondered why he'd never noticed that Dana and the other women he'd dated were such shallow people.

Then a sobering thought hit him with a solid blow. Had *he* been as self-serving and self-involved as the women in his life? Glancing down at the baby daughter who had changed his world and his life so completely, Brian felt a sudden rush of gratitude for whatever forces had brought her to him. Since Maegan, he had found not only a deep, abiding love for his child, but he'd found something else, as well.

Something that he hadn't even realized he'd been missing. A mental image of Kathy Tate rose up in his mind. Quickly he compared the warm, loving, *real* woman he'd come to care for so deeply to Dana and knew there was no contest.

Maegan began fussing again, so Brian gave her swing a little push as he continued to think about his future. *Their* future. He was more certain now than ever before that he wanted Kathy Tate in his life. Not just because she was a wonderful mother to his daughter.

But because he couldn't imagine waking up in the morning and *not* seeing her face.

Now all he had to do was find a way to convince Kathy that they belonged together. Forever.

Eleven

By the time Brian and Maegan came home from the park, Kathy had walked at least a hundred miles, pacing off the steps in the small confines of her apartment. She'd tried to work. Had promised Tina she would finish the stack of résumés in time to be delivered tomorrow.

But the reality of the situation was she hadn't been able to think of anything but Brian. And Maegan. And the prospect of losing the two people who had come to mean so much to her. She'd been thinking all morning, racking her brain in an effort to find a solution to all of their problems.

And as she listened to the familiar sounds of Brian's footsteps in the hallway, she realized that she *did* have the answer. If she had the nerve to go through with it, and if Brian would agree.

Hurriedly crossing the room, she threw open her door just as Brian unlocked his. He turned to look at her, a soft smile on his face. Maegan, her hair full of sand, her overalls damp, reached out two chubby arms toward her, and Kathy swallowed hard. This had to work, she told herself. For all their sakes, this had to work.

"Hi," Brian said. "We missed you at the park."

Kathy smiled and stepped forward to pluck Maegan from his grasp. Enjoying the feel of two small hands patting her cheeks, she said, "I missed you guys, too."

He opened his door and waved her inside. "Want to come in?"

"Yeah," Kathy said and took one small step that brought her up close to him.

Brian reached out and brushed a stray lock of her hair behind her ear, and goose bumps raced along her flesh in response. Would he always be able to do that to her with a simple touch?

"Did you get your work done?" he asked, his voice dropping a notch or two into an intimate rumble that sent her blood pressure skyrocketing.

She tipped her head back to look up at him. Staring into those blue eyes of his, she admitted, "No."

"Why not?"

"Too busy thinking."

"About me?" he asked hopefully.

"You," she said. "And me. And Maegan. Us."

"Any conclusions?"

"One or two." Good heavens, how was she supposed to convince him of her plan when she couldn't seem to string more than three or four words together at a time?

"I've come to a couple of conclusions myself," he said, and he let his fingers trail down along the length of her arm, from shoulder to waist.

Kathy buried the shiver building inside her and stepped past him into the apartment. "We have to talk."

"It's as good a place as any to start." He followed her in, closing the door behind him.

Walking across the living room, Kathy set Maegan down on the floor in the center of a ring of toys. Then slowly she straightened up and turned around to face the man who dominated her thoughts so completely these days.

"Kathy…"

"Let me go first," she said, interrupting him quickly. "I've got to say this fast."

He nodded. "Okay." Then, crossing his arms over his chest, he watched her and waited.

Suddenly nervous, Kathy started pacing again. She walked in a wide circle around Maegan, who clapped her hands as if in approval of a new game. Giving the baby a distracted smile, Kathy glanced at Brian and said, "I've been thinking.…"

He smiled. "You said that already."

"I know." Lifting both hands in an eloquent shrug, she continued. "What you said last night. About deployment. I mean…you have to have someone you trust and someone she knows to leave Maegan with.''

''Yeah…?''

''And, well. I love her, and I think she loves me.''

''I know she does.''

Kathy grinned at him briefly. ''Thanks.'' She sucked in a deep breath and rushed on before she could stop herself. ''Anyway, the point of all this is, I think I have a plan that will solve everything.''

''Which is…?''

Here was the tough part, she thought, stiffening her spine as if she was facing a firing squad. Heck, all she needed to complete the picture was a blindfold and a cigarette. *Ready…aim…fire!* ''We should get married. You and me, I mean. Not Maegan and me. I mean—'' she blew out a breath ''—marry me.''

Brian's eyes widened until she thought they might pop from his head and roll across the floor. Not exactly the response she'd been hoping for.

''Are you serious?'' he asked.

''Plenty serious,'' she told him, nodding. ''I would *never* joke about getting married. I mean, think about it. It's the answer to all of our problems.''

He shook his head as if to clear it. ''But last night you told me you never wanted to get married. You said your mom—''

''Yeah, I know,'' she interrupted him again, knowing she was being rude, and beyond caring. ''But this would be different.''

''How?''

She shoved both hands into the back pockets of her

jeans. "Think of this more like a business proposition than a real marriage."

He took a step closer, then stopped again. "Business."

"Exactly."

"Uh-huh," he said, his gaze locked with hers. "Explain?"

"Well," she started slowly, her words picking up speed as her brilliant idea coalesced in her mind. "What I'm actually proposing is a sort of marriage of convenience."

"Sounds romantic."

"That's the point, though," she said quickly. "Romantic marriages, those based on *love* just don't last. Believe me, I've seen enough of them to know. But this would be a real partnership, Brian."

"Go on," he said, though he didn't sound at all happy so far.

Still, at least he was listening.

"If we get married, I'll be there to take care of *our* daughter," she said, and loved the sound of those two words. "When you're deployed, you wouldn't have to worry about her at all."

"Uh-huh."

"And when you're at home, we'd be together." And this was a big plus in her book. "The two of us could enjoy *wonderful* sex, and neither one of us would have to risk our hearts on something as elusive as *love.*"

Of course, the idea of marriage at all was still terrifying to her. But Kathy truly believed she'd found a way to take all the risk out of it. She'd always wanted a family. Children. If Brian agreed to her plan, she could actually have everything she'd ever wanted. Along with the one thing she'd never counted on finding—the magic she'd discovered in Brian's arms.

And as long as she hid the fact that she loved him, he would never have the power to hurt her. It was perfect, she thought, hoping to high heaven that he would see that, too.

Brian just stared at her. All the way home he'd tried to come up with a way to propose and get her to accept it. He'd finally decided to just tell her he loved her, demand she marry him and *order* her to trust him enough not to hurt her.

Wouldn't you know she'd find a way to pull the rug out from under him?

And she looked so blasted pleased with herself. Oh, she was nervous; he could tell that from the way she rocked back and forth on her heels. But the flush on her cheeks and the glimmer in her eyes let him know she thought this whole marriage-without-love thing was a great idea.

Maybe it could have been, he thought, if he didn't already love her like crazy. Everything inside him railed against the idea of a loveless marriage. He wanted more from her than a business deal. He wanted her heart. Her love.

For the first time in his life he wanted what his parents had had. What both of his sisters had. A loving marriage. A family.

And he wanted all of that with Kathy.

He gazed at her for a long, thoughtful moment, reminding himself that she was taking a big chance here. He knew how she felt about marriage, and a part of him understood her fears. But damn it, if a couple went into a marriage with low expectations, what were the chances that they'd find happiness?

"What do you think?" she asked, and her voice sounded hushed, strained.

He thought they were both nuts, that's what he thought. And he thought they should be on their knees thanking Whoever had brought them together instead of talking about dissecting the magic of their relationship and stuffing it into a glass bottle labeled Business Deal.

But in the next instant he realized that if he said exactly what he was thinking, Kathy would cut and run. It would finally be strike three, and he'd be out. Some nameless marine would win the pool they were running on the base and Brian would be alone. He and Maegan both would lose the one woman who could make them both happy.

Kathy was nervous enough about marriage to turn her back on him and Maegan forever rather than risk her heart. And having her in his life this way would be better than spending his life without her.

So before he could change his mind and push her for what she wasn't ready to give, he heard himself say, "I think it's a great idea."

She heaved a relieved sigh, and Brian's heart twisted a little. Then she practically ran at him, throwing her arms around his neck and pressing the length of her body against his.

Drawing her head back, she looked up at him and smiled. "It'll be great, Brian. You'll see."

"Sure it will, baby," he said and wrapped both arms around her, holding her to him with a viselike pressure. His body stirred, and his blood heated to the boiling point. He let one of his hands slide down to caress the curve of her backside and she hummed throatily in pleasure. She might say she didn't want love, but what they had meant more to her than simple sexual delight. She loved him, damn it. All he had to do was convince her of that.

They'd get married, he thought. And he'd let her think it was all just business, if that was the only way to get her to say I do. But once their marriage was legal, he was going to find a way to show her that love wasn't something to be afraid of. And that what they could have together was something that only came around once in a lifetime.

"So," he asked, giving her another quick squeeze, "when do you want to do it?"

She moved one hand to cup the back of his head, and just the touch of her fingers against his scalp had him breathless. "I thought about that, too."

He wasn't surprised.

"My mom's getting married in Vegas next weekend," she said.

"I remember. And?"

She shrugged and reached up to plant a quick kiss at the corner of his mouth. "And I thought we could drive out for the wedding, then get married ourselves.''

A one-week engagement and a Vegas wedding. His mother would kill him. But the sooner he made Kathy his wife, the sooner he could start his campaign to win her love.

''Another brilliant idea,'' he said, and gave her the smile he knew she wanted.

Kathy moved her hands to cup his face. Staring up at him, she said quietly, ''We'll be a family, Brian. You, me and Maegan.''

''A family,'' he repeated, and felt a warm glow flicker to life inside him. He wanted them all to be a *real* family. The three of them…and, surprisingly enough, he wanted more children with Kathy. He didn't want Maegan to grow up an only child. But so much of this depended on his ability to reach Kathy. To make her see that love was nothing to be afraid of.

A flash of doubt shone briefly in her eyes and quickly disappeared again. ''This is the right thing to do, isn't it?''

If he'd needed any persuading to marry her fast, before she could change her mind, that question would have done it. He bent his head and kissed her, hard and long and deep. His tongue moved over her lips and through them, into the warm recesses of her mouth.

Her hands shifted to his shoulders and gripped hard.

And after a long, intimate moment, he pulled his head back, looked her square in the eyes and said honestly, "This is absolutely, without a doubt, the most right thing either one of us will ever do."

Three days later, after an exhausting, eight-hour shopping safari, Kathy had finally found the right dress to be married in. As she steered her Volkswagen toward home, she imagined the look on Brian's face when he saw her in the ivory dress. A shiver ran up her spine, and a slow burning heat began to build inside her.

"I still can't believe you're actually getting married," Tina said from the seat beside her.

Kathy threw a quick look at her and grinned. She was having a hard time believing it herself. In less than a week she would be a wife. And a mother. Heady thoughts for a woman who'd vowed never to say I do. Yet hadn't she quivered a minute ago, just thinking about the man? "I am, though. In four short days."

"And I don't get to be there."

"We've been through this," Kathy said on a sigh.

"Yeah, yeah. I know. It's a business arrangement." She snorted a disbelieving laugh.

"It *is*," Kathy told her firmly. The one thing allowing her to go through with this was the knowledge that a marriage of convenience would protect her heart.

"What did your mom say to all this?"

"She was…surprised." To say the least. When she'd called her mother the night before, Kathy had tried to explain the situation, but naturally, all Spring wanted to hear were the "romantic details" of her daughter's courtship and whirlwind marriage.

"I'll bet she was," Tina said.

"All right, so Spring doesn't understand." Kathy stopped for a red light and turned her head to look at her best friend. "But I was really hoping you would."

"What I understand," Tina said quietly, "is that you're trying to fool yourself into believing that you can marry the man you love and pretend it's all business."

Wounded, Kathy turned her gaze back to the intersection in front of her. She could do it, she told herself. She *had* to do it.

"Tell me something," Tina said.

"What?"

"Why did you exhaust us both searching for the perfect dress if this wedding is no big deal?"

Because she wanted to make Brian's jaw drop when he saw her. But if she said that, undoubtedly Tina would read something more into it. "Whatever the reason, I am getting married. I didn't want to do it in jeans and a T-shirt."

"Uh-huh." Tina shook her head and looked out the passenger side window. "Whatever you say, Kath."

Tina was bound and determined to throw love into this mixture. And Kathy was just as determined to keep love out of it. If she felt more for Brian than she was willing to admit, that would be her secret. With a marriage of convenience, she could have everything she'd ever wanted. And she wouldn't run the risk of being devastated one day, when he decided to leave her for greener pastures.

"At least I get to meet him," Tina said. "That's something, I guess."

Nodding, Kathy forced a smile and said, "I promise. When we get back, we'll get baby-sitters for the kids and go out to dinner. You and Ted and me and Brian."

"You're on, and as my wedding present, I'll arrange for the sitter."

"Thanks, pal."

Tina grinned and winked. "I'll even watch the baby myself for a long weekend if you and Brian want to have to short honeymoon. Or no…" She paused and shook her head. "A business arrangement doesn't require a honeymoon, does it?"

"Very funny," Kathy said, and turned onto her street. "But I'll have you know that sex is a part of our bargain."

"How very mature of you both."

She knew sarcasm when she heard it. "There's no reason to deprive ourselves of…"

"Love?" Tina supplied the word.

"Sex," Kathy corrected her.

"Honey," her friend said as she parked the car in front of the apartment building, "where there's sex, there's fire and where there's fire, business contracts tend to get burned up."

Kathy shut off the engine and set the brake. "You'll see. This is going to work perfectly."

As she got out of the car, she thought she heard the

other woman mutter, "Sounds like 'famous last words' to me." She ignored her friend and pulled her wedding dress from the back seat. It *was* going to work. It had to. And nothing was going to spoil this for her. She'd taken care of everything.

"I still can't believe you're getting married," the gorgeous brunette said as she picked up her purse and headed for the front door.

"Why does everyone say that?" Brian wondered aloud.

"You figure it out, gunny," she answered on a laugh. "All I know for sure is, Jack says the guys are fit to be tied because you ruined the pool."

"Ahh…" he said with a smile, picturing all of his fellow marines coming up empty because they'd bet on him to strike out. "Yet another good reason for getting married."

"I'm sorry I didn't get to meet her," Donna Harris said, "but at least I got another look at your daughter."

"And?" Brian asked, waiting for the compliments that were definitely Maegan's due.

"*And*, she's beautiful."

"Looks like her father," he said, and knew he was sounding like an idiot. But he couldn't seem to help himself. Ever since accepting Kathy's proposal, he'd been so damned happy, he half expected someone on base to shoot him just for being annoying.

Opening the door for his guest, Brian stood aside as Donna stepped through into the hallway. But before she could leave, he swept her into a hard hug. "Thanks," he said.

"For what?"

"For baby-sitting. And, oh, for marrying Jack and giving me such a good example."

"You're welcome," Donna said on a laugh.

Brian grinned and gave her a quick kiss on the cheek.

It was only then he noticed that the narrow hallway wasn't empty. Kathy and another woman were staring at him, and if looks could kill, he would have dropped dead on the spot. In the next instant Kathy headed for her apartment, blatantly ignoring him and Donna.

He knew how this looked, though, and he wasn't about to let her go on thinking what she was obviously thinking. Snagging Kathy's arm as she passed him, he turned her around and said a bit too cheerfully, "Hi, honey, glad you got home in time to meet a friend of mine."

Kathy could hardly breathe. And for the first time Brian's touch hadn't lit a trail of warmth inside her. Instead, she felt icy cold. Seeing the other woman in Brian's arms had been enough to clamp an invisible fist around her heart. And now he wanted to introduce her to the woman he'd only just kissed with easy familiarity?

Kathy felt as though she'd been slapped. Pain blossomed inside her chest and radiated throughout her body, making her legs tremble and her breath come in short, furious gasps. Not only was he cheating on her before they were even married, he had the guts to actually expect her to make polite small talk.

"This is Donna Harris," he was talking fast now. "She's the wife of my best friend, Jack. Also the daughter of Colonel Candello."

Beside her, Tina practically oozed relief. Kathy knew that logically she should be feeling the same thing. Unfortunately, logic didn't seem to have a lot to do with what she was feeling at the moment.

But she smiled, anyway, said all the right things and even managed a polite chuckle or two. She introduced Tina to both Brian and Donna, and after several long, uncomfortable moments, the two women left together, and Brian and Kathy were alone in the hallway.

It was all very innocent, she told herself. So why didn't she feel better? Why was there a knot the size of Cleveland in the pit of her stomach?

She couldn't look at him. If she did, he would see the pain still shimmering in her eyes. "I've got some things to do," she said lamely, and unlocked her door. "I'll see you later, okay?"

"Kathy—"

"Later, all right?" God, she had to get away from him. Had to think. Had to stop the pain that continued to ebb and flow inside her. She gave him one long, last look, then she stepped into the apartment and closed the door behind her.

Damn it, Brian thought, no. Not later. Now. Going back into his own apartment long enough to pick up the baby, he crossed the hall and knocked at her door.

"Go away, Brian," she said, her voice muffled and strangely thick sounding.

"I'm not going away, Kathy," he said. "I'm going to stand right here knocking until you open the door and talk to me."

She opened it a moment later and looked up at him. Her mouth worked furiously, as if she was holding back tears. Instantly he knew she was still hurt by what she'd thought she'd seen. "Kathy," he said, and slipped inside before she could bar his entry, "I know what that looked like, but it was perfectly innocent. You know that now."

"Yes," she said quietly, looking from him to Maegan and back again. Then she sniffed and lifted her chin. "I know that now."

"So tell me what you're thinking."

"I told you I needed some time alone."

"Time alone isn't going to fix this. We need to talk about it."

She inhaled sharply and blew air out in a rush. "I know you want to talk…"

"But?" he asked, hearing her unspoken hesitation and bracing for the worst.

"But it doesn't matter," she said.

"What do you mean, it doesn't matter?" His grip on Maegan tightened, and the baby squirmed against him in protest.

"Talking won't change anything," she said tightly.

"Won't change what?" he forced himself to ask,

despite having the decided feeling that he wasn't going to like what she had to say.

"This just isn't going to work," she muttered, more to herself than to him. "I really thought it would, but it won't. Can't."

Keeping his gaze fixed on her wounded eyes, Brian asked bluntly, "What are you trying to say?"

"The only thing I can say. The wedding's off, Brian," she said, and he felt each of her words hit him with the impact of a bullet.

Twelve

"**A**re you out of your mind?" he demanded in a bellow just below the noise level of an air-raid siren.

She shook her head fiercely. "Shouting at me won't change my mind."

"What will?" Brian ground out stiffly.

"Nothing," she said, and walked past him into the center of the apartment. Wrapping her arms around herself, she held on tightly and looked at him. She seemed so...lost his heart ached for her. The warm, cozy familiarity of the apartment was almost mocking him now. There was no warmth here anymore. Just one man fighting to hold on to the woman who'd come to mean so much to him.

"I was wrong," she said, and her voice shook

slightly. She bit down on her bottom lip. "I thought if I pretended our marriage wasn't *real,* I could avoid being hurt. Now I know differently."

"Kathy," he said, and took two steps closer to her. She shook her head wildly and backed up a pace to keep him at a distance. Renewed pain and frustration sliced at him. "What you saw was nothing."

"It doesn't matter, don't you see?"

"No," he said abruptly. "I don't."

"When I saw you and Donna…together…I knew. I knew that, pretend marriage or not," she said as a single tear rolled down her cheek, "if you cheated on me, or left me, I'd be devastated."

"If? You're willing to throw away what we have on an *if?*" This couldn't be happening, he told himself. She was a smart woman. She wouldn't do this. No matter what her childhood had been like.

"I have to. I won't put myself—or you and Maegan—through the kind of pain a divorce brings. I just won't." As hard as this was, and she felt as though her heart was actually splintering in her chest, Kathy knew it was easier than what they might face in the future. If she had married him, built a life with him and then lost it, it would have killed her. Right now, she was maimed. But she would survive, darn it.

Maegan, reacting to the emotions coloring the air, reached out both arms to her, and what was left of Kathy's heart dissolved. God, she was losing everything. Brian. Maegan. And the fleeting hope of a family.

Instinctively she went to him and plucked the baby

from his arms. Cuddling her close, she cooed soft words and snatches of half-remembered melodies in an effort to soothe both Maegan and herself. It wasn't working.

Teary-eyed, she looked up at Brian. Seeing the devastation in his eyes almost convinced her to change her mind. But she strengthened her resolve. Best to end it now before they were both in it so deep there would be no living through the pain of an ending.

"I think it would be better," she said brokenly, "if we just didn't see each other anymore."

"Just like that," he said, and she heard the tightly leashed fury in his voice.

"It'll be easier on all of us," Kathy said even though she knew that nothing about this was easy. "Maybe your friend Donna will watch Maegan for you until you can find someone else."

"Yeah," he said, and Kathy risked another glance at him. His features were hard, and she finally saw him as the professional warrior she knew him to be. "She probably will."

She nodded, though her heart was breaking. Some other woman would be loving *her* baby. Someone else would watch her smiles, dry her tears and see all the little miracles she would perform while growing up.

And someday, she thought, though her mind fought against going there, some other woman would lie in the shelter of Brian's arms and find the magic she'd discovered such a short time ago.

Oh, God, could a person live with a shattered heart?

Giving the baby a kiss, Kathy whispered, "Goodbye, sweetheart,'' before she could give in to the urge to grab on to Brian and hang on. Then she handed her back to her father. Kathy's arms had never felt emptier. She'd never felt so cold.

"Okay, I'll go,'' Brian said, "because I can see that talking to you now isn't going to do a damn bit of good.''

She nodded gratefully.

"But before I go, there's a few things you ought to know.'' Patting the baby's back gently, he straightened up to his full, imposing height and looked down at Kathy through eyes so icy it was a wonder she didn't get frostbite. "You say you're doing all this because I might cheat. Hurt you.''

Kathy swallowed hard and kept her gaze locked with his. "Yes.''

"Lady, when I make a promise, I *keep* it. My word means something to me.'' He took a step closer, and Kathy felt anger and disappointment and frustration pouring from him in cold waves. "If I swear to be faithful to you, then, by damn, I'm faithful. But saying it doesn't mean squat if you can't trust me.''

"That's not what this is about,'' she interrupted.

His eyes flashed. "That's *exactly* what this is about.'' Shock roared through him, and Brian took a tight rein on the temper boiling inside. The woman he loved was throwing away everything they'd found together because of what *might* go wrong years down the line. And there didn't seem to be a damn thing he could do about it.

Well, screw it. At least he'd go down fighting.

"Y'know something, Kathy?" he asked. "You're a coward."

She hiccuped. "What?"

"A coward. You're hiding from what we might have because you don't want to take the risk of being hurt." He sucked in a deep gulp of air, kept one hand on Maegan's back and continued. "Well, welcome to the world, honey. *Everybody* gets hurt from time to time. That's part of living. And if you're not taking risks, then you're not living." Shaking his head, he added, "Ignoring love doesn't mean it's not there. It just means you're missing the best parts of life."

She didn't say anything, just stared up at him through those brown eyes he knew would be haunting him.

Hopeless, he thought. This was all hopeless. Turning around, he headed for the door, but when he got there, he stopped and looked back at her. "You know, I've been avoiding saying something that I should have said the first time I laid eyes on you."

"Brian…" She shook her head as if she could stop him from uttering the words. She couldn't.

"I love you, damn it." He stabbed his index finger in the air, pointing at her. "And you love me."

"It's not about love."

"Of course it is," he said on a choked-off snort of derision. "And here's something else for you to chew on when you think about all this. You're feeling like this only because of the way you grew up."

She stiffened.

"Well, I can't do anything about the hurts you had

as a kid, but I want you to know something. I *admire* your mother.''

''What?''

She looked completely confused now, so Brian cleared it up for her.

''That's right. I admire her. Because no matter how many times she's been disappointed by love, she's never stopped looking for it.'' His voice dropped to a low, husky note as he added, ''And, honey, that's a better way to live than hiding from love entirely.''

Then he was gone and Kathy was alone again.

''Man,'' Jack Harris snapped, ''if you don't lighten up I'm going to see what I can do about arranging a firing squad.''

Lighten up? Brian felt as if he was drowning in a sea of darkness. He hadn't seen Kathy since she'd called off their wedding, hoping that their separation might work in his favor. But apparently, she was made of sterner stuff than he was. Because although missing her was driving him nuts, she hadn't cracked.

''Her mother's wedding's tomorrow,'' Brian said as he continued to pace the tiny confines of their office. ''Hell, *we* were supposed to get married tomorrow.''

''So?''

Brian shot the other man a glare that should have fried him. *''So?''*

''So, what are you gonna do about it?'' Jack leaned back in his chair and looked at him.

''I'll tell you what I want to do.''

''Besides punch me, you mean?''

Not just Jack, he thought. He wanted to punch walls, faces, doors. Anything. But there was something else he wanted far more.

"Yeah. I want to fly to Vegas, hog-tie her and *force* her to marry me."

"Ahh. A plan destined to win any woman's heart."

"I've already got her heart, damn it," Brian said furiously. It was driving him nuts knowing that she loved him and still wouldn't marry him.

"Then it seems to me something drastic is called for."

"Like?"

"Well," Jack said, a smug smile on his face, "when Donna tried to leave me, I followed her to the airport and carried her back home where she belonged."

Brian remembered. Their fellow marines had teased Jack unmercifully, calling him "my hero" for weeks. But Jack hadn't cared. He had Donna and that's all he'd been interested in. "But you were already married."

He shrugged. "Vegas is full of chapels."

"Yeah," Brian said softly, thinking fondly of the idea. "Maybe what I have to do here is order a full-frontal assault on her defenses."

"So you're not ready to call strike three?" Jack asked, hiding a smile. "The guys will be disappointed."

"Strike three?" Brian grinned for the first time in days. "Hell, boy, I'm about to smack a grand slam!" Then he headed for the door.

Behind him, he heard Jack holler, "Ooh-rah!"

* * *

Kathy hadn't known there was that much pain in the world. A dull, throbbing ache in the spot where her heart used to be had been her constant companion the past few days. She missed Maegan desperately. And not having Brian in her life was pure torture.

So what had she accomplished by cutting him out of her life? No future pain could be worse than what she was already suffering. Basically, in order to save herself pain, she'd given herself pain.

Brilliant.

"Oh, honey, I'm so glad you're here," her mother said, and Kathy forced her attentions back on the coming wedding.

"Me, too, Mom." Actually, Kathy thought as she looked at her mother, Spring looked different than she had at any of her other nuptials. The older woman was actually *glowing* in anticipation of reciting the vows she had to know by heart.

"I know I've said this before," Spring said ruefully, "but I really believe that this time it's going to be different. This time it's forever." She shifted her gaze to watch her groom approach, and even Kathy could see the shine in her mother's eyes.

Frank Butler stopped alongside Spring, threaded her arm through his and looked at Kathy through kind eyes. "Your being here means a lot to your mother," her about-to-be new stepfather said, "and to me."

"I wouldn't have missed it," Kathy said, and studied the man. Frank Butler wasn't what she had expected. About sixty, he had a well-developed paunch, a hairline that had receded to the back of his head—and he looked at Spring as if she were the most beautiful woman in the world.

Maybe it would be different this time, Kathy thought hopefully. Maybe her mom really had found happiness at last.

As the couple took their places at the altar, Kathy stepped into a pew and watched, only half listening to the ceremony. Brian's words kept echoing over and over again in her mind, and she finally acknowledged that he'd been right. About a lot of things.

She *was* a coward. Her eyes teared as she watched her mom exchange rings with her new husband and realized with a start that, as Brian had said, Spring had never stopped looking for love. And wasn't that a better way to live than actually finding love and throwing it away because you were afraid you might lose it?

Here she sat, wearing the pretty ivory dress she'd picked as her wedding outfit. Kathy ran the flat of her hand over the lace-edged skirt and sighed. A wedding dress and no wedding. How depressing was that?

Could the pain of turning your back on love be any less than losing it? Good heavens, her mother had spent her whole life looking for what Kathy had found and tossed aside.

Her mind spinning, Kathy smiled at her mother as the newlyweds retreated down the aisle. She tried to follow them, but her feet wouldn't move. She felt as though she was stuck in cement. Her gaze flitted over the tacky furnishings of the Love Me Tender Wedding

Chapel, and all she could think was, If she hadn't been so stupid, she and Brian would be standing at that altar right now.

They'd have been a family. She would have been with the man she loved. She would have been a mother. She would have had everything she'd ever dreamed of. Instead she was alone and she had no one but herself to blame.

Knees weak, brain racing, Kathy at last forced herself out of the pew and toward the exit. Somehow she'd find the words to congratulate her mother—and maybe even apologize for not understanding her before. Then, if it wasn't too late, she'd go home and talk to Brian.

Maybe he missed her as much as she missed him. Maybe he'd be willing to forgive her for being so stupid and hardheaded. And maybe she'd get a second chance.

She stepped into the Vegas sunshine and blinked at the brightness. Before her eyes were used to the light, she walked smack into a familiar broad chest, and only a strong hand on her forearm kept her from falling.

"Brian?" she whispered, half wondering if her broken heart had summoned up his image just to torture her.

"This has gone on long enough," he said in a growl that let her know immediately this was no vision.

"It is you," she said, and felt her heart begin to beat again for the first time since telling him goodbye.

"Of course it's me," he said, and when the baby gurgled, he added, "and Maegan."

"And Maegan," Kathy repeated, feeling a bubble of laughter rise up inside her. She felt so light, so full of wonder and happiness she was amazed she didn't simply float off the sidewalk.

It didn't matter to her *why* he was there. The important thing was he'd come.

"Aren't you going to ask why we're here?" he demanded.

If he wanted her to, okay by her.

"Sure," she said, grinning up at him. She couldn't stop smiling. Didn't want to stop smiling. "Why are you here?"

He frowned at her and paused for a long moment. Apparently, he'd had his speech all worked out and she was throwing him a loop.

"Kathy?" her mother said.

"Mom, this is Brian Haley and his daughter, Maegan." She never took her eyes off the tall marine in full uniform. "Brian, this is my mom, Spring, and my stepfather, Frank."

He glanced their way and said, "Nice to meet you, folks." Then he handed Maegan to a surprised Spring. "Would you mind, ma'am."

"Not at all," she said, and immediately jiggled the little girl while keeping her interested gaze fixed on her daughter and the marine.

Brian set both hands on Kathy's shoulders and pulled her so close that she was forced to tilt her head right back just to look at him. He'd been planning this speech for hours, but now that he was here, he knew the most important thing in the world was just to kiss her.

Bending his head, he took her mouth in a deep, soul-searing kiss that branded her as completely as it did him. As if he was leaving his last mark on the earth, he gave her everything he had to give and tried to tell her without words just what she meant to him. And after a small eternity passed, he lifted his head and looked down into her dazed, brown eyes.

"Oh, Brian…"

"Nope," he said quickly, interrupting her. "My turn to talk."

"But…" She smiled and Brian's heart ached.

"I'm here for one reason, Kathy," he said lightly. "I *love* you and you love me. And you'd damn well better get used to the idea."

She opened her mouth to talk, but he cut her off. He hadn't liked the idea of driving all the way to Vegas, just him and the baby, so he'd taken an early flight out of John Wayne airport, listened to Maegan crying the whole trip, risked their lives in a Vegas taxicab, and he wasn't about to stop talking until he'd convinced her.

"You can't deny what we have, Kathy," he said, letting his gaze sweep across her features. God, he'd missed her in the past few days. Being without her had been like missing a limb. She was a part of him. So deep a part, he couldn't imagine a world where they weren't together. "And I won't let you toss it aside. Understand me, honey. I'm a marine, and we don't know the meaning of the word *retreat*. And,'' he added as she tried to talk again, ''let me remind you that I'm a gunnery sergeant. I have all kinds of weapons and soldiers I can call on to help me convince you.''

''Brian...''

''We're getting married, honey. Now. Today.''

Spring gasped.

Kathy blinked.

Maegan laughed.

''A *real* marriage, Kathy. No business deals. No easy-out clauses,'' he said ''The real thing. With love and kids and dogs and whatever the hell else a marriage is. Happily ever after, amen.''

''If you'll just let me say something—''

''I mean it, Kath,'' he continued, his fingers tightening on her shoulders, ''we're not leaving this damn town until we're married. Now, we can walk into that chapel side by side, or I can carry you.'' He took a breath, blew it out and asked, ''Which'll it be?''

''Are you finished?'' Kathy asked, smiling up at him.

''For the moment,'' he said, watching her warily.

''Good, then I have something to say,'' she told him.

He nodded and kept watching her. She noted that he didn't let her go, either. Which was just fine by her.

Kathy looked up at him and wondered how she could ever have thought she could live without him. She needed Brian Haley in her life as much as she needed air and water. He'd given her so much more than she'd ever hoped to find. And she wanted it all, right down to the "happily ever after."

Worrying about possible pain in a distant future just wasn't a good enough reason to give up so much happiness now.

Later she'd tell him all of that. Right now she settled for saying, "Carry me, Gunnery Sergeant."

Relief flooded his features, and he gave her that crooked smile that would always touch her heart. Then he bent down, swept her up into his arms and said, "Yes, ma'am."

Glancing back at her mother, Kathy asked, "Will you be my matron of honor, Mom?"

Spring kissed her new granddaughter and grinned at her own little girl. "Oh, sweetie, I'd be proud to."

Kathy smiled, then wrapped her arms around her almost husband. How had she ever gotten so lucky? "So, what are we standing around here for? Let's get this wedding started."

"You're my kind of woman, honey," he said in a voice so deep it reached into every corner of her soul and warmed her through. And Kathy knew, no matter what, she would never be cold again.

Brian lifted her high enough for a quick kiss and breathed easily for the first time in too many days. He'd been given a second chance, not only at being a daddy, but at a love deeper than he'd ever dreamed possible. And he wasn't about to blow either of them.

Shouting, "Ooh-rah!" he marched into the chapel, relishing the sound of Kathy's laughter in his ears.

* * * * *

Celebrate the joy of bringing a baby into the world—
and the power of passionate love—with

A BOUQUET OF BABIES

An anthology containing three delightful stories
from three beloved authors!

THE WAY HOME
The classic tale from *New York Times* bestselling author

LINDA HOWARD

FAMILY BY FATE
A brand-new Maternity Row story by

PAULA DETMER RIGGS

BABY ON HER DOORSTEP
A brand-new Twins on the Doorstep story by

STELLA BAGWELL

Available in April 2000, at your favorite retail outlet.

Silhouette®
Where love comes alive™

If you enjoyed what you just read,
then we've got an offer you can't resist!

Take 2 bestselling love stories FREE!
Plus get a FREE surprise gift!

Clip this page and mail it to Silhouette Reader Service™

IN U.S.A.
3010 Walden Ave.
P.O. Box 1867
Buffalo, N.Y. 14240-1867

IN CANADA
P.O. Box 609
Fort Erie, Ontario
L2A 5X3

YES! Please send me 2 free Silhouette Desire® novels and my free surprise gift. Then send me 6 brand-new novels every month, which I will receive months before they're available in stores. In the U.S.A., bill me at the bargain price of $3.12 plus 25¢ delivery per book and applicable sales tax, if any*. In Canada, bill me at the bargain price of $3.49 plus 25¢ delivery per book and applicable taxes**. That's the complete price and a savings of over 10% off the cover prices—what a great deal! I understand that accepting the 2 free books and gift places me under no obligation ever to buy any books. I can always return a shipment and cancel at any time. Even if I never buy another book from Silhouette, the 2 free books and gift are mine to keep forever. So why not take us up on our invitation. You'll be glad you did!

225 SEN CNFA
326 SEN CNFC

Name	(PLEASE PRINT)	
Address	Apt.#	
City	State/Prov.	Zip/Postal Code

* Terms and prices subject to change without notice. Sales tax applicable in N.Y.
** Canadian residents will be charged applicable provincial taxes and GST.
   All orders subject to approval. Offer limited to one per household.
   ® are registered trademarks of Harlequin Enterprises Limited.

DES99   ©1998 Harlequin Enterprises Limited

New York Times **Bestselling Author**

LINDA LAEL MILLER

Wild About Harry

Harry Griffith is not an impulsive man. But when the Australian businessman meets Amy, the lovely young widow of his best friend, he suddenly finds himself doing all sorts of irrational things. Caught in the emotional whirlwind Harry's creating, Amy wants to give in to the passion she feels. But trapped by the bittersweet memories of the husband she lost, Amy isn't sure what her future holds. In fact, the only thing she's sure of is that she's wild about Harry.

"Sensuality, passion, excitement…
are Ms. Miller's hallmarks."
—*Romantic Times*

Available mid-March 2000 wherever paperbacks are sold!

SILHOUETTE'S 20TH ANNIVERSARY CONTEST
OFFICIAL RULES
NO PURCHASE NECESSARY TO ENTER

1. To enter, follow directions published in the offer to which you are responding. Contest begins 1/1/00 and ends on 8/24/00 (the "Promotion Period"). Method of entry may vary. Mailed entries must be postmarked by 8/24/00, and received by 8/31/00.

2. During the Promotion Period, the Contest may be presented via the Internet. Entry via the Internet may be restricted to residents of certain geographic areas that are disclosed on the Web site. To enter via the Internet, if you are a resident of a geographic area in which Internet entry is permissible, follow the directions displayed on-line, including typing your essay of 100 words or fewer telling us "Where In The World Your Love Will Come Alive." On-line entries must be received by 11:59 p.m. Eastern Standard time on 8/24/00. Limit one e-mail entry per person, household and e-mail address per day, per presentation. If you are a resident of a geographic area in which entry via the Internet is permissible, you may, in lieu of submitting an entry on-line, enter by mail, by hand-printing your name, address, telephone number and contest number/name on an 8"x 11" plain piece of paper and telling us in 100 words or fewer "Where In The World Your Love Will Come Alive," and mailing via first-class mail to: Silhouette 20th Anniversary Contest, (in the U.S.) P.O. Box 9069, Buffalo, NY 14269-9069; (In Canada) P.O. Box 637, Fort Erie, Ontario, Canada L2A 5X3. Limit one 8"x 11" mailed entry per person, household and e-mail address per day. On-line and/or 8"x 11" mailed entries received from persons residing in geographic areas in which Internet entry is not permissible will be disqualified. No liability is assumed for lost, late, incomplete, inaccurate, nondelivered or misdirected mail, or misdirected e-mail, for technical, hardware or software failures of any kind, lost or unavailable network connection, or failed, incomplete, garbled or delayed computer transmission or any human error which may occur in the receipt or processing of the entries in the contest.

3. Essays will be judged by a panel of members of the Silhouette editorial and marketing staff based on the following criteria:

   Sincerity (believability, credibility)—50%

   Originality (freshness, creativity)—30%

   Aptness (appropriateness to contest ideas)—20%

   Purchase or acceptance of a product offer does not improve your chances of winning. In the event of a tie, duplicate prizes will be awarded.

4. All entries become the property of Harlequin Enterprises Ltd., and will not be returned. Winner will be determined no later than 10/31/00 and will be notified by mail. Grand Prize winner will be required to sign and return Affidavit of Eligibility within 15 days of receipt of notification. Noncompliance within the time period may result in disqualification and an alternative winner may be selected. All municipal, provincial, federal, state and local laws and regulations apply. Contest open only to residents of the U.S. and Canada who are 18 years of age or older, and is void wherever prohibited by law. Internet entry is restricted solely to residents of those geographical areas in which Internet entry is permissible. Employees of Torstar Corp., their affiliates, agents and members of their immediate families are not eligible. Taxes on the prizes are the sole responsibility of winners. Entry and acceptance of any prize offered constitutes permission to use winner's name, photograph or other likeness for the purposes of advertising, trade and promotion on behalf of Torstar Corp. without further compensation to the winner, unless prohibited by law. Torstar Corp and D.L. Blair, Inc., their parents, affiliates and subsidiaries, are not responsible for errors in printing or electronic presentation of contest or entries. In the event of printing or other errors which may result in unintended prize values or duplication of prizes, all affected contest materials or entries shall be null and void. If for any reason the Internet portion of the contest is not capable of running as planned, including infection by computer virus, bugs, tampering, unauthorized intervention, fraud, technical failures, or any other causes beyond the control of Torstar Corp. which corrupt or affect the administration, secrecy, fairness, integrity or proper conduct of the contest, Torstar Corp. reserves the right, at its sole discretion, to disqualify any individual who tampers with the entry process and to cancel, terminate, modify or suspend the contest or the Internet portion thereof. In the event of a dispute regarding an on-line entry, the entry will be deemed submitted by the authorized holder of the e-mail account submitted at the time of entry. Authorized account holder is defined as the natural person who is assigned to an e-mail address by an Internet access provider, on-line service provider or other organization that is responsible for arranging e-mail address for the domain associated with the submitted e-mail address.

5. Prizes: Grand Prize—a $10,000 vacation to anywhere in the world. Travelers (at least one must be 18 years of age or older) or parent or guardian if one traveler is a minor, must sign and return a Release of Liability prior to departure. Travel must be completed by December 31, 2001, and is subject to space and accommodations availability. Two hundred (200) Second Prizes—a two-book limited edition autographed collector set from one of the Silhouette Anniversary authors: Nora Roberts, Diana Palmer, Linda Howard or Annette Broadrick (value $10.00 each set). All prizes are valued in U.S. dollars.

6. For a list of winners (available after 10/31/00), send a self-addressed, stamped envelope to: Harlequin Silhouette 20th Anniversary Winners, P.O. Box 4200, Blair, NE 68009-4200.

Contest sponsored by Torstar Corp., P.O. Box 9042, Buffalo, NY 14269-9042.

ENTER FOR
A CHANCE TO WIN*

Silhouette's 20ᵗʰ Anniversary Contest

Tell Us Where in the World
You Would Like *Your* Love To Come Alive...
And We'll Send the Lucky Winner There!

Silhouette wants to take you wherever
your happy ending can come true.

Here's how to enter: Tell us, in 100 words or less,
where you want to go to make your love come alive!

In addition to the grand prize, there will be 200
runner-up prizes, collector's-edition book sets
autographed by one of the Silhouette anniversary
authors: **Nora Roberts, Diana Palmer,
Linda Howard** or **Annette Broadrick**.

DON'T MISS YOUR CHANCE TO WIN!
ENTER NOW! No Purchase Necessary

Silhouette®

Where love comes alive™

Name:

Address:

City: State/Province:

Zip/Postal Code:

Mail to Harlequin Books: **In the U.S.**: P.O. Box 9069, Buffalo, NY
14269-9069; **In Canada**: P.O. Box 637, Fort Erie, Ontario, L4A 5X3

*No purchase necessary—for contest details send a self-addressed stamped envelope to:
Silhouette's 20ᵗʰ Anniversary Contest, P.O. Box 9069, Buffalo, NY, 14269-9069 (include
contest name on self-addressed envelope). Residents of Washington and Vermont may
omit postage. Open to Cdn. (excluding Quebec) and U.S. residents who are 18 or over.
Void where prohibited. Contest ends August 31, 2000.

PS20CON_R